P9-CCI-137

Sunny

Diary Two

**Other books by
Ann M. Martin**

Leo the Magnificat
Rachel Parker, Kindergarten Show-off
Eleven Kids, One Summer
Ma and Pa Dracula
Yours Turly, Shirley
Ten Kids, No Pets
Slam Book
Just a Summer Romance
Missing Since Monday
With You and Without You
Me and Katie (the Pest)
Stage Fright
Inside Out
Bummer Summer

THE KIDS IN MS. COLMAN'S CLASS series
BABY-SITTERS LITTLE SISTER series
THE BABY-SITTERS CLUB mysteries
THE BABY-SITTERS CLUB series
CALIFORNIA DIARIES series

California Diaries #6

Sunny

Diary Two

Ann M. Martin

SCHOLASTIC INC.
New York Toronto London Auckland Sydney
Mexico City New Delhi Hong Kong Buenos Aires

No part of this publication may be reproduced in whole or in part,
or stored in a retrieval system, or transmitted in any form or by any means,
electronic, mechanical, photocopying, recording, or otherwise,
without written permission of the publisher.
For information regarding permission, write to Scholastic Inc.,
Attention: Permissions Department, 557 Broadway, New York, NY 10012.

Copyright © 1998 by Ann M. Martin.
All rights reserved. Published by Scholastic Inc.
Printed in the U.S.A.

ISBN 0-439-12362-3
(meets NASTA specifications)

SCHOLASTIC, READ 180, CALIFORNIA DIARIES, and associated logos
and designs are trademarks and/or registered trademarks of Scholastic Inc.
LEXILE is a trademark of MetaMetrics, Inc.

14 15   23   13 12

*The author gratefully acknowledges
Peter Lerangis
for his help in
preparing this manuscript.*

FRIDAY 3/13
6:00 P.M.

JUST GOT BACK FROM VISITING MOM AT THE HOSPITAL.

GOD, I AM TIRED OF WRITING THAT.
I KNOW. I'LL WRITE IT A HUNDRED TIMES.
THEN I CAN CUT AND PASTE. SAVE SOME ENERGY.

JUST GOT BACK FROM VISITING MOM AT THE HOSPITAL.
JUST GOT BACK FROM

NO. I'LL HAVE A <u>STAMP</u> MADE. MUCH EASIER.

NEVER MIND.
I'M NOT IN THE MOOD TO WRITE.

SATURDAY 3/14
4:04 A.M.

MOM JUST CALLED.
SHE ASKED ME IF I COULD BRING HER THE
<u>PALO CITY POST</u>.

At
4
in
the
morning.

I told her, uh, we don't get it for another two hours.

She kind of freaked. She apologized about a hundred times. She said she must be losing her mind. She thought it was already tonight.

I had to calm her down. I told her the phone did not wake anyone but me — which is a lie, because I hear someone walking around in the kitchen. I also said she couldn't be losing her mind. If she were, she wouldn't have remembered I was staying at Dawn's house.

That didn't convince her.

Doesn't convince me either.

Mom is slipping.

I mean, the hair loss and weight loss were bad enough. But we expected that.

Not the mind, though. Lung cancer isn't supposed to affect the brain.

I don't understand this. All the hospital

VISITS, ALL THE CHEMO AND RADIATION — THEY'RE ALL SUPPOSED TO HELP. BUT THEY'RE NOT. SHE'S JUST GETTING WORSE AND WORSE. PLUS SHE'S EXHAUSTED FROM ALL THE TRIPS TO THE HOSPITAL.

FACE IT, WINSLOW.

READ BETWEEN THE LINES.

DR. MERWIN HAS STOPPED TALKING ABOUT "GOOD SIGNS."

THERE ARE NO GOOD SIGNS.

SHE'S NOT GOING TO GET BETTER.

SO WHAT'S THE POINT? DAD SHOULD JUST TAKE HER AWAY FROM THAT HORRIBLE PLACE, BRING HER BACK HOME WHERE SHE'LL BE COMFORTABLE. TAKE CARE OF HER.

IN SICKNESS AND IN HEALTH. ISN'T THAT WHAT THEY SAY AT WEDDINGS?

DAD WOULDN'T REMEMBER. HE ONLY REMEMBERS SALES FIGURES. EVERYTHING'S THE STORE, THE STORE, THE STORE. WHAT'S HE GOING TO DO WHEN THE STORE IS ALL HE HAS?

TILL DEATH DO US PART. THAT'S THE OTHER THING THEY SAY.

THE TRUTH IS, MOM WOULD BE BETTER OFF DYING AT HOME.

THERE.

I SAID IT.

AND I'M NOT SORRY.

WHY DO I DO THIS TO MYSELF?

I AM STAYING AT DAWN'S TO ESCAPE. I'M
NOT SUPPOSED TO GET ALL WORKED UP.

WHY DO I BOTHER WRITING IN THIS THING?
THIS DOESN'T HELP MY INSOMNIA!

I AM CRAZY, THAT'S WHY. I NOT ONLY HAVE A
MISERABLE, DEPRESSING LIFE, BUT I WRITE ABOUT
IT. JUST TO MAKE MYSELF FEEL WORSE.

AND WHAT'S DAWN DOING? SNORING.
DREAMING ABOUT HAPPY DAWN STUFF, PROBABLY.
A PERFECT WORLD, WITH LOTS OF FLOWERS BUT NO
ALLERGIES. ANIMALS ROAMING FREELY ON THE
STREETS. PEOPLE GIVING UP THEIR CARS, RIDING
BIKES TO WORK, PICKING BERRIES AND VEGETABLES
FOR LUNCH. PEACE ON EARTH. WHATEVER.

I LOVE HER.

I REALLY DO.

DAWN, IF YOU FIND THIS AND ARE PEEKING AT
THIS PAGE, THAT PARAGRAPH WAS A JOKE. I LOVE
YOU!

SHE IS MY BEST FRIEND. SHE LETS ME STAY
AT HER HOUSE. IF I COULDN'T DO THAT, IF I HAD
TO BE HOME EVERY DAY, I'D BE A NUTCASE.

I HAVE TO BE KIND TO HER.

EVEN IF SHE SNORES.

I HAVE NUDGED HER A FEW TIMES. THAT SHUTS HER UP FOR, OH, 30 SECONDS. THEN SHE STARTS UP, LOUDER THAN EVER.

I CAN'T STAY IN THIS ROOM.

I KNOW WHAT I HAVE TO DO.

EAT.

4:32

BAD BAD BAD IDEA.

I THINK I HAVE PERMANENTLY LOST MY APPETITE.

CAROL WAS PUTTERING AROUND IN THE KITCHEN. WELL, MAYBE NOT PUTTERING. WITH THAT BIG OLD PREGNANT BELLY, IT WAS MORE LIKE LUMBERING.

I WAS RELIEVED. ANY OTHER GROWN-UP WOULD HAVE YELLED AT ME FOR BEING UP SO LATE. BUT CAROL WAS . . . CAROL. 32 GOING ON 15. "INSOMNIA TOO?" SHE SAID. "COOL, LET'S HAVE A MIDNIGHT SNACK."

WHICH SOUNDED GREAT. I MEAN, IF I HAD TO HAVE COMPANY WHILE I WAS AWAKE, IT MIGHT AS WELL BE SOMEONE I LIKE.

So Carol began chatting away about her pregnancy and her crazy appetite, and about how she had to "eat for two" now.

I politely went along. I took a plastic container of leftover Chinese food out of the fridge. I put it on the table, ready to inhale it.

And then I saw what Carol was eating.

Tuna fish.

And chocolate.

Together.

She was standing there, blabbering away, with strands of stringy brown glop stuck between her teeth.

Back into the fridge went the Chinese food. And here I am again. In bed, listening to Dawn's snores.

At least I'm not hungry.

Now I can't eat or sleep.

Oh, well. I'll just stay awake. I'll fill up this journal. I'll fill 2 journals. Ms. Newell will be so impressed. Maybe I'll even pass English.

I can publish it. The Incredible Revolting Life of Sunshine Daydream Winslow, A Memoir.

Oh. I forgot. We have to keep these

JOURNALS PRIVATE. NO ONE IS EVER SUPPOSED TO SEE THEM. THAT'S PART OF THE VISTA SCHOOL EXPERIENCE.

SO WHAT HAPPENS IF YOU SHOW THEM TO SOMEONE? YOU FLUNK?

I THINK CHRIS HAS THE RIGHT IDEA. JUST FILL YOUR PAGES WITH RANDOM WORDS. "PEAS CARROTS RABBITS PIGS OINK THUNDER AND LIGHTNING," STUFF LIKE THAT. WHY KNOCK YOURSELF OUT IF THE TEACHERS AREN'T GOING TO READ IT?

CHRIS IS SO FUNNY. CUTE AND FUNNY.

CHRIS.

I LIKE WRITING HIS NAME.

CHRIS.

I'M FEELING BETTER ALREADY.

CHRIS?

OH.

MY.

GOD.

WHAT AM I GOING TO DO WHEN HE COMES OVER TOMORROW NIGHT? NOT TOMORROW — TONIGHT! I'LL HAVE BAGS UNDER MY EYES. I'LL BE STAGGERING WITH FATIGUE. I'LL LOOK LIKE MOM.

HOW IRONIC. MAYBE I SHOULD SAY I HAVE CANCER. THAT'S A GOOD EXCUSE.

HEY, IT WORKS FOR MOM.

I DIDN'T WRITE THAT.

I DID WRITE THAT.

I DISGUST MYSELF.

SATURDAY
9:46 A.M.

I DID IT.

I ACTUALLY SLEPT.

I THINK.

IT FELT LIKE SLEEP, ANYWAY. A SORT OF WAKEY KIND OF SLEEP. FULL OF NIGHTMARES.

WHATEVER IT WAS, IT'S OVER.

DAD JUST CALLED.

NOTHING LIKE A FEW WORDS FROM PAUL WINSLOW TO GET THE MORNING OFF TO A BAD START.

FIRST HE REMINDED ME THAT I HAVE MY OWN BED AT MY OWN HOUSE, AND MAYBE I SHOULD SPEND A FEW NIGHTS AT HOME INSTEAD OF SPONGING OFF DAWN'S DAD AND STEPMOM.

WELL, HE DIDN'T ACTUALLY SAY "SPONGING," BUT THAT'S WHAT HE MEANT.

THEN HE DROPPED THE BIG NEWS: HE WAS SHORTHANDED AT THE STORE.

I SHOULD HAVE TOLD HIM TO GROW ANOTHER
HAND. I SHOULD HAVE TOLD HIM SOMETHING. BUT I
DIDN'T. My BRAIN WAS FRIED FROM LACK OF SLEEP.
So GUESS WHERE I HAVE TO GO NOW?
TO WINSLOW BOOKS. TO WORK.
FOR FREE.
WITH THE BOSS FROM HELL.
DEAR OLD DAD.

SATURDAY
12:25 P.M.

LUNCH BREAK.
A SLEEP BREAK WOULD BE BETTER. FAT
CHANCE FOR THAT.
I AM HUDDLED IN THE CORNER OF WINSLOW
BOOKS. EARTH SCIENCES TO THE LEFT. ENGINEERING
TO THE RIGHT.
NO ONE WILL BOTHER ME HERE. I HOPE.
So. GUESS WHY I HAVE TO WORK ON A
SATURDAY WHEN I HAVE A BIG DATE COMING UP
AND I COULDN'T SLEEP THE NIGHT BEFORE?
BECAUSE ONE OF DAD'S CLERKS QUIT. AGAIN. THIS
GUY DIDN'T EVEN GIVE NOTICE. HE JUST CALLED UP
AND SAID HE WASN'T COMING IN ANYMORE.

NEEDLESS TO SAY, DAD IS ON THE WARPATH.

DAD IS <u>ALWAYS</u> ON THE WARPATH ABOUT SOMETHING.

MAYBE IF HE GOT OFF IT, HIS CLERKS WOULDN'T QUIT ALL THE TIME.

YOU KNOW WHAT I WISH?

I WISH THAT DAD AND MOM COULD CHANGE PLACES. JUST FOR A DAY.

THAT SOUNDS AWFUL.

NO, I DON'T WANT DAD TO HAVE LUNG CANCER.

I JUST WANT HIM TO FEEL WHAT <u>REAL</u> PROBLEMS ARE LIKE.

SATURDAY
6:14 P.M.

WHY CAN'T HE <u>LEAVE ME ALONE</u>?

I WAS MINDING MY OWN BUSINESS. I WAS SHELVING BOOKS, EXACTLY WHAT HE ASKED ME TO DO.

DID I <u>KNOW</u> I WASN'T SUPPOSED TO BE LISTENING TO MY RADIO? DID I <u>KNOW</u> ONE OF THE CUSTOMERS WAS OFFENDED? WOULD I HAVE DONE IT IF I <u>DID</u> KNOW?

He had no right to blow up at me in front of the whole store!

He's lucky I slave for him. He's lucky he HAS me.

I don't deserve this treatment.

I don't deserve this life.

I should have run away from home when I had the chance.

I blew it with Carson that time at Venice Beach. I never should have told him I was 13. I should have lied and said 16. That's only a year younger than him. He would have believed me, I know it. He would have let me travel across the country with him. We'd probably be in some cool place by now, like the Rockies or New York City.

But no. He had to leave me all alone. Jerk.

Well, I'm a jerk too. I could have run away on my own. Hopped a bus. Hitched a ride. Something.

But I didn't. I came crying home. And now I'm paying for it.

Let's see what Chris is like. Hey, I can always run away with him.

If he ever gets here.

10:02 P.M.

Maybe it's destiny. Maybe this was just meant to be the worst date of my entire life.

It started out fine. Chris looked so cool when he picked me up. All excited and happy. "You ready?" was the first thing he said.

"Ready for ANYTHING," I replied.

He drove through the streets with the convertible top down. We were shouting at the pedestrians. Having a great time.

I was hoping for the beach. I would have settled for less, though. A movie. Dinner out. The arcade. A walk in Las Palmas County Park. Even just the parking lot. Something fun.

Then he looked at his watch and said, "Whoa, the game starts in five minutes," and I figured, okay, we're going to the baseball park.

But no.

He drove to his house. And I had to run after him as he rushed inside. Why?

To catch the basketball game between the Chicago Bulls and the Los Angeles Lakers.

ON TV!

THAT WAS OUR DATE — SITTING WITH HIS DAD
AND SOME STALE CHIPS AND SALSA IN FRONT OF
THE TUBE.

HE SAID HE'D ALREADY WARNED ME ABOUT IT.
(HE'S LYING.) HE INSISTED IT'S THE BIGGEST GAME
OF THE YEAR. HE ACTED LIKE I WAS SUPPOSED TO
THANK HIM.

SO WHAT COULD I DO? I WAS TRAPPED.

HIS PARENTS WERE REALLY NICE TO ME. THEY
GAVE ME LOTS OF SNACKS AND DRINKS. AND CHRIS
KEPT TRYING TO EXPLAIN THE RULES OF THE GAME.

BUT AFTER AWHILE EVERYONE WAS IGNORING ME.
THEY WERE TOO BUSY SHOUTING AT THE SCREEN
AND GETTING MAD BECAUSE THE BULLS WERE
KILLING THE LAKERS.

SO I DID THE ONLY THING THAT MADE SENSE.
I CHEERED FOR THE BULLS.

WHY NOT? THEY WERE WINNING. BESIDES, THEIR
TEAM IS MUCH BETTER-LOOKING. SO ARE THEIR
UNIFORM COLORS.

I WAS ONLY TRYING TO LIVEN THINGS UP.
CHRIS DIDN'T HAVE TO GET SO FURIOUS AT ME.
FRANKLY, I DON'T CARE ANYMORE.
CHRIS IS HISTORY.

I SLEPT.

END OF GOOD NEWS.

THE BAD NEWS?

WHILE I WAS WITH WHAT'S-HIS-NAME LAST NIGHT, I WAS SUPPOSED TO BE VISITING MOM AT THE HOSPITAL.

SHE CALLED DAWN'S HOUSE, TRYING TO REACH ME.

DAWN FELT SORRY FOR MOM, SO SHE WENT TO VISIT. IN MY PLACE.

THAT IS SO DAWN.

I GUESS SHE MEANT WELL. BUT I FEEL WEIRD. I MEAN, HOW DOES THAT LOOK TO MOM — HER OWN DAUGHTER FORGETS, BUT HER DAUGHTER'S BEST FRIEND SHOWS UP?

DAWN LOOKED KIND OF ANNOYED WHEN SHE TOLD ME THIS. EVERYTHING I DO THESE DAYS SEEMS TO ANNOY HER.

GUESS IT'S TOUGH BEING PERFECT.

I WAS IN NO MOOD TO BE SCOLDED. SO THE MOMENT DAWN STARTED IN, I WALKED AWAY.

"YOU'RE WELCOME," SHE CALLED OUT.

"SORRY," I SAID. "I MEAN, THANKS."

WHO NEEDED THIS? I SAID GOOD-BYE AND MADE A REALLY DUMB DECISION — I DECIDED TO LEAVE AND HAVE BREAKFAST AT HOME.

I MEAN, WHAT DID I THINK — DAD WOULDN'T KNOW ABOUT MY MISSED VISIT?

"HAVE FUN LAST NIGHT?" HE ASKED AS I WALKED INTO THE HOUSE.

"I KNOW, I FORGOT," I SAID.

"I REMINDED YOU A THOUSAND TIMES YESTERDAY!"

WHICH COULD BE TRUE. HE PROBABLY YELLED IT AT THE TOP OF HIS LUNGS, IN THE MIDDLE OF THE STORE IN FRONT OF EVERYBODY. ALONG WITH A MILLION OTHER THINGS I TUNED OUT.

I TOLD HIM TO CHILL. I MEAN, WHAT IS THE BIG DEAL? MOM PROBABLY DIDN'T NOTICE. SHE'S IN A LOT OF PAIN. VISITORS MAKE HER TIRED. MAYBE DAWN'S VISIT WAS A BURDEN.

COULD DAD UNDERSTAND THAT CONCEPT? NOPE. I HAD TO STAND THERE AND LISTEN TO ALL THE WAYS I WAS A ROTTEN, IRRESPONSIBLE PERSON.

AGAIN.

I GUESS THE OPINION IS UNANIMOUS.

SCHOOL. HOME. WORK. DAWN'S HOUSE.

FINE.

I DON'T NEED ANY OF THEM.

WHICH IS THE MAIN REASON I AM AT THE BUS STATION RIGHT NOW.

MAYBE I'LL GO TO THE BEACH.

NO. BETTER IDEA. I'LL GO TO DUCKY'S, AND HE CAN <u>DRIVE</u> ME TO THE BEACH.

MISERY LOVES COMPANY.

I DID IT!

I FOUND HIM!

WHO'S HIM?

HIM IS BROCK.

YES, BROCK. COOL NAME.

I FOUND HIM AT THE BEACH. EATING A BURRITO AT THE CAFE.

I LOVE BURRITOS. ESPECIALLY WHEN THEY'RE IN THE HANDS OF A BRONZE GOD WITH GREAT ABS.

HE WAS LOOKING AWAY FROM ME AS I SAT DOWN. AND THE BURRITO WAS JUST HANGING THERE. THE INSIDES LOOKED ABOUT READY TO FALL ONTO THE BENCH.

SO I TOOK A BITE.

DUCKY COULD NOT BELIEVE IT. HE LOOKED AT ME IN TOTAL SHOCK.

BUT IT GOT BROCK'S ATTENTION.

I POINTED TO THE BURRITO AND SAID, "THANK YOU."

HE WASN'T OFFENDED. HE SMILED AND ANSWERED, "YOU'RE WELCOME."

THEN I ASKED HIM IF HE WANTED MY PHONE NUMBER.

I THOUGHT DUCKY WAS GOING TO FALL OFF THE BENCH IN A FAINT.

AND GUESS WHAT? HE SAID YES AND GAVE ME HIS. (I MEAN, DUH. IF YOU WANT SOMETHING, ASK FOR IT, THAT'S MY MOTTO.)

WELL, DUCKY RECOVERED. IN FACT, HE WAS THE ONE WHO INVITED BROCK TO SIT WITH US ON THE BEACH.

DUCKY IS THE BEST FRIEND.

ANY OTHER TYPICAL GUY WOULD HAVE BEEN SO JEALOUS — ESPECIALLY IF HE'D CHANGED ALL HIS PLANS JUST TO GO TO THE BEACH, THE WAY DUCKY DID. HE WAS SUPPOSED TO HELP HIS BROTHER PAINT THEIR GARAGE TODAY — BUT THE MOMENT I CAME OVER AND MENTIONED THE BEACH, HE BEGAN PACKING A COOLER AND STUFFING A BLANKET AND TOWELS INTO HIS BACKPACK.

HE IS MORE THAN A BEST FRIEND. HE'S A SAINT.

SAINT DUCKY THE GREAT

THANK YOU. BLESS YOU.

OOPS. I SHOWED MY PRIVATE JOURNAL TO SOMEONE! TSK-TSK.

WHERE WAS I? OH, YES. SO BROCK SAID OF COURSE HE WOULD LOVE TO SIT WITH US BECAUSE HE COULDN'T RESIST MY MELTING SMILE AND DEEP, SEXY EYES.

WELL, HE SAID YES, ANYWAY. HE JUST THOUGHT THE REST.

DUCKY LUGGED ALL THAT STUFF TO A SUNNY SPOT FAR AWAY FROM THE CROWD, WHERE WE COULD HAVE A LITTLE PRIVACY.

BROCK AND I HAD THE BEST TIME. WE SWAM. PLAYED VOLLEYBALL. BURIED EACH OTHER IN SAND.

AND THE BEST NEWS IS — HE GOES TO VISTA! WHICH I KIND OF KNEW, BECAUSE I HAVE SEEN HIM IN THE HALLWAYS.

HE'S NOT MUCH OF A TALKER. BUT TALK DIDN'T MATTER. WE COMMUNICATED WITH OUR EYES.

I AM THE WOMAN OF HIS DREAMS. I KNOW IT. AND I WON'T LET HIM FORGET IT.

I HAVE HIS PHONE NUMBER.

10:37 P.M.

I DECIDED TO SLEEP AT HOME. BE ALONE WITH MY THOUGHTS.

It could have been a perfect rest-of-the-day.

It wasn't.

Dawn had to spoil it.

She left a message on the answering machine. Asking me something about the English exam.

I called back and asked, "What exam?"

Dawn was not pleased. She said Ms. Newell announced it last Tuesday.

I think that was the day I cut class to be with Chris.

It's HIS fault.

Dawn was all concerned. She wanted me to come over and study with her.

I said thanks but no thanks.

I can always cut English tomorrow too.

Monday 3/16
9:45

Greetings from Las Palmas County Park.

I'm not supposed to be here now.

I'm supposed to be in science.

But I got sidetracked this morning. By

THE TIME I HEADED FOR SCHOOL, I WAS ALREADY
LATE FOR HOMEROOM. SO I HAD TWO CHOICES:

1. RUSH TO HOMEROOM, BE SCREAMED AT BY
MR. LEAVITT, GO TO SCIENCE, THEN CUT ENGLISH.
   OR
2. DON'T BOTHER. ENJOY LIFE FOR AWHILE,
THEN SLIP INTO SCHOOL FOR THIRD PERIOD, AFTER
ENGLISH.

THIS WAS A NO-BRAINER.

IT'S NOT LIKE I TRIED TO BE LATE. IT'S
DAD'S FAULT.

DAD'S AND CAROL'S AND JANE FONDA'S.

OKAY, HERE'S THE STORY. I WAS EATING
BREAKFAST AND DAD RACED INTO THE KITCHEN, ALL
GRUMPY AND RUSHED. HE SAID MOM HAD ASKED HIM
FOR SOME OLD PHOTO ALBUMS TO LOOK AT, BUT
HE HADN'T HAD TIME TO GET THEM.

ROBO SLAVE DAUGHTER TO THE RESCUE. AS
USUAL. RIGHT IN THE MIDDLE OF MY FROSTED
SHREDDED WHEATS, I WENT UP TO MOM'S
BOOKSHELF.

I DIDN'T EXPECT TO FIND MY BABY BOOK
TUCKED AWAY THERE. I DIDN'T KNOW I HAD A
BABY BOOK.

SO I READ THROUGH IT. I FOUND A LOCK OF
MY HAIR PASTED INTO THE BOOK — AND IT WAS

MOUSE BROWN! THEN I SAW THIS INCREDIBLE
PHOTO. AT FIRST I THOUGHT IT HAD BEEN TAKEN
RECENTLY, BECAUSE MOM'S LYING IN A HOSPITAL
BED, ALL TIRED AND RAGGED-LOOKING. BUT SHE'S
SMILING. RADIANT. PLUS SHE HAS ALL HER HAIR,
AND SHE'S HOLDING THIS SCREAMING LITTLE NEWBORN,
ME. I'M WRAPPED IN A WHITE COTTON BLANKET,
AND MY FACE LOOKS DISGUSTING, ALL SCRUNCHED UP
AND RED.

But I WASN'T REALLY LOOKING AT ME.

I COULDN'T TAKE MY EYES AWAY FROM MOM.
IT WAS AS IF SHE WERE ALIVE, RIGHT THERE IN MY
HANDS. TALKING TO ME. TELLING ME SHE WAS
HAPPY, AND EVERYTHING WAS GOING TO BE OKAY.

IT WAS LIKE SEEING SOMEONE I HAVEN'T SEEN
IN YEARS.

I HAD TO STOP LOOKING AT IT. IT MADE ME
FEEL ALL KNOTTED UP INSIDE.

So I RIPPED THE PICTURE OUT AND PUT IT
IN MY POCKET.

I'LL SHOW IT TO MOM ON MY NEXT VISIT.

ANYWAY, AS I WAS TAKING DOWN THE PHOTO
ALBUMS, I SAW MOM'S OLD JANE FONDA
PREGNANCY WORKOUT VIDEO ON THE SHELF.

I MEAN OLD. THE COVER IS HILARIOUS. ALL

THESE HUGE WOMEN IN LEOTARDS AND DORKY HAIRSTYLES BOUNCING AROUND.

I FIGURED, HEY, MOM'S NOT GOING TO USE THIS ANYMORE. BUT IT WAS PERFECT FOR CAROL.

SO I LEFT THE ALBUMS ON THE KITCHEN TABLE FOR DAD. AND TOOK THE VIDEO TO THE SCHAFERS'.

CAROL, OF COURSE, WENT NUTS OVER IT. SHE HUGGED ME AND SAID A MILLION THANK-YOUS.

I THOUGHT I'D CATCH DAWN, BUT SHE'D LEFT FOR SCHOOL ALREADY. AS I STARTED TO GO, CAROL PUT ON THE TAPE.

THEN SHE STARTED EXERCISING ALONG, AND I THOUGHT SHE WAS GOING TO KILL HERSELF. THE EXERCISES WERE FOR EARLY PREGNANCY. I COULD NOT LEAVE THE HOUSE. I RAN IN AND FAST-FORWARDED TO THE LATE SECTION. I MEAN, SHE IS 7 MONTHS! YOU DON'T GET MUCH LATER THAN THAT.

THEN I SAW IT. THE LOOK ON CAROL'S FACE.

IT WAS A LOT LIKE THE LOOK ON MOM'S FACE IN THE PICTURE.

THAT WAS WHEN I LEFT.

BIG NEWS.

SAW BROCK IN THE GYM HALLWAY. BEFORE 7TH PERIOD. DON'T USUALLY TAKE THAT ROUTE. WILL FROM NOW ON.

HE WAS ALL SWEATY FROM PLAYING BASKETBALL, HIS HAIR IN LITTLE WET RINGLETS.

I SAID HI. HE SAID HI.

I TALKED ALL ABOUT THE CHICAGO BULLS — AND GUESS WHAT? HE LOVES THEM.

I CAN ALWAYS SPOT A GUY WITH GOOD TASTE.

HE WALKED ME TO CLASS, AND WE TALKED AND TALKED — WELL, I DID. I WAS KIND OF BLABBERING. I WAS HOPING HE'D ASK ME OUT, BUT HE DIDN'T.

SO I ASKED HIM.

SUNNY "GUTS TO SPARE" WINSLOW.

AND GUESS WHAT?

HE. SAID. YES.

LATER

POOR DUCKY. HE LOOKED SO SAD AFTER SCHOOL. I THOUGHT HE WAS ABOUT TO CRY. I

GRABBED HIM AND SAT HIM DOWN BY THE BIG
PALM TREE OUTSIDE SCHOOL.

    I WAS WORRIED. I THOUGHT IT WAS SOMETHING
SERIOUS.

    BUT IT WAS JUST THE USUAL STUFF ABOUT HIS
FRIEND ALEX — ALEX IS DEPRESSED, DUCKY'S
WORRIED HE'S GOING TO DO SOMETHING "RASH,"
BLAH BLAH BLAH.

    I TRIED TO LISTEN. BUT FRANKLY, THIS IS SO
<u>OLD.</u> I TOLD DUCKY HE DESERVED BETTER FRIENDS
THAN ALEX. THE GUY IS A DRIP. A LOSER. I
MEAN, IF I WERE HIS BEST FRIEND, BY NOW I'D
HAVE ONLY 3 WORDS FOR HIM: GET A LIFE.

Anyway, I was BURSTING to tell him my news about Brock.

I may have cut him off. I probably should have paid more attention.

But this is important. To me, at least.

Friday's only three days away, and I needed Ducky's fashion advice.

WEDNESDAY 3/18
5:15 P.M.

I know what a ghost looks like.

It doesn't smile like Casper. But it does wear a white gown.

It has wispy white hair, papery gray skin, and large purple circles under its eyes.

It looks out the window when you're talking. It doesn't eat. It is cold to the touch, and you can feel its bones through its skin.

It forgets the topic of conversation in the middle of sentences. It doesn't recognize the photo you show it. It keeps asking the same questions over and over.

And you hate seeing it, because it breaks your heart.

I WENT HOME AFTER THE HOSPITAL VISIT, BUT I COULDN'T GO INSIDE.

DAD'S CAR WASN'T THERE, AND I DIDN'T FEEL LIKE BEING IN AN EMPTY HOUSE.

SO I WENT OVER TO DAWN'S.

WHEN CAROL ANSWERED THE DOOR, I SMILED AND SAID HI. I THOUGHT I WAS BEING MY CHEERFUL OLD SELF.

BUT THE MINUTE SHE SAW ME, HER FACE FELL. "WHAT HAPPENED TO YOU?" WAS THE FIRST THING SHE SAID.

NO OSCARS IN MY FUTURE, HUH?

WE SAT IN THE LIVING ROOM, AND I TOLD HER A LITTLE BIT ABOUT THE VISIT. I DIDN'T WANT TO MAKE A BIG DEAL. I REALLY DIDN'T WANT TO TALK ABOUT IT AT ALL.

BUT AS I WAS TALKING, DAWN CAME IN AND STARTED ASKING QUESTIONS.

NEXT THING I KNEW, MR. SCHAFER WAS THERE, AND THEN JEFF, STANDING IN THE ARCHWAY.

I CLAMMED UP.

I DID NOT NEED THE SNOTTY COMMENTS OF MY BEST FRIEND'S SNOTTY LITTLE BROTHER.

FOR AWHILE, NO ONE SAID ANYTHING. THEN

Jeff spoke up, in a soft voice. "My friend's hamster died. His little brother ran over it with a toy fire truck."

Mr. Schafer ushered Jeff out of the room. Carol started apologizing for him.

I wasn't angry, though. I could tell Jeff was trying to be helpful, in his own weird way.

I tried to say that, but Carol cut me off. She grabbed my hand. "You poor, poor thing," she said.

Dawn nodded. "It's been hard for you."

I kept telling them I was fine. And I was. But they were shaking their heads sadly and telling me I could cry if I needed to.

"It's all right to feel what you're feeling, you know," Dawn informed me.

"No kidding," I muttered. "I mean, how can you NOT feel what you're feeling?"

Dawn scowled. "I was only trying to help."

I hated the way they were looking at me. As if I were some pathetic stray dog at the pound.

"Sorry," I said, getting up to leave. "I have to go home."

The baby is kicking.

Carol let me feel it (him? her?) this morning. I stopped by the Schafers' on the way to school, and Carol made me put my face right up to her tummy. At first I couldn't feel a thing.

Then she told me to sing.

So I sang the first song that popped into my head. My absolute favorite Maggie Blume tune — "Hey, Down There."

Appropriate, I thought.

BAM. A sharp toe, right to the kisser.

I screamed. It was the WEIRDEST feeling.

Carol was laughing. She said the baby's going to be a soccer player.

Dawn made me swear I'll never tell Maggie what happened. That song is her pride and joy.

Carol stood in the doorway, waving to us as we walked off. Her other hand rested on her belly.

She looked so cool.

I don't know what it is about pregnant women. They just have this GLOW.

I told that to Dawn. She gave me a funny look. She said Carol always glows. Carol has oily skin.

Ouch. So catty.

"You still don't like her, huh?" I asked.

"What do you mean?" Dawn said. "Of course I do. She's my stepmother."

"Well, you didn't at first. And sometimes you still seem — I don't know, a little angry at her."

"You have a big imagination, Sunny."

Fine.

Maybe she's right.

I have to see this from her point of view.

Must be kind of strange, to see your stepmom carrying your dad's child. Especially when your mom is still alive.

Am I going to feel that way too, if Dad remarries?

Guess I have to start thinking about stuff like that.

4:10 P.M.

WHY WHY WHY DO I HATE BEING HERE SO MUCH?

WHY DO I FEEL SICK?

WHY DO I FEEL LIKE I'M GOING TO FAINT?

I'VE BEEN HERE A MILLION TIMES. I SHOULD BE USED TO IT BY NOW.

I AM VISITING MOM.

I AM HER DAUGHTER.

I SHOULD BE LOVING AND SUPPORTIVE AND INTERESTED AND SYMPATHETIC.

AND ALL I CAN THINK OF IS GETTING OUT OF HERE.

I KNOW WHY.

IT'S DAWN.

I SHOULD NEVER HAVE COME WITH HER.

DAWN THE DEVOTED. DAWN THE PERFECT AND PERKY.

HOW. CAN. SHE. BE. SO. UP?

"HI, MRS. WINSLOW. YOU'RE LOOKING SO PRETTY, MRS. WINSLOW. IS THERE ANYTHING I CAN DO FOR YOU, MRS. WINSLOW? COME ON, SUNNY, LET'S PROP UP THE BED/CALL THE NURSE/GET YOUR MOM SOME FOOD/TELL HER ABOUT SCHOOL TODAY."

And now she's in the bathroom, helping Mom, while I'm out here feeling like a jerk.

I should be with Mom. I would be too if my best friend weren't such a Girl Scout.

I want to help. But whenever I'm about to offer it, Dawn speaks up first.

When that ugly nurse came in and thought Dawn was Mom's daughter, I wanted to scream. What did she think I was — her secretary?

Okay. Calm down.

NO. BIG. DEAL.

Why am I so jumpy?

I will never understand myself.

I wish Ducky were here. He calms me down.

Oh, well. He should be pulling into the parking lot any minute. With Maggie and Amalia. Just in time for our shopping spree.

Maybe Dawn won't come with us.

Maybe she'll decide to stay on as Mom's personal aide.

Maybe Mom will adopt her.

Dawn and I can switch. I'll become a Schafer, she'll be a Winslow.

Nahh. I wouldn't wish that fate on Dawn.

There's the latch on the bathroom door.

Time to go.

8:04 P.M.

T MINUS TWENTY-FOUR HOURS.

TONIGHT THE VISTA HILLS MALL. TOMORROW
BROCK!

IT TOOK FOREVER TO FIND THE RIGHT OUTFIT.

I THOUGHT MY FRIENDS WOULD HELP ME. BUT
NO. DAWN KEPT PICKING OUT THESE FRILLY, LACY,
WHITE SUMMER DRESSES. STUFF THAT WOULD LOOK
GOOD ON HER.

MAGGIE THINKS I SHOULD GO '70s. LIKE,
ORANGE BELL BOTTOMS AND BEADS. I KEPT SAYING
NO TO ALL HER SUGGESTIONS. SHE KEPT TELLING
ME, "BUT IT'S ALL ON SALE!"

PLEASE. DOES THE PHRASE LAST YEAR
MEAN ANYTHING? NO ONE DRESSES LIKE THAT
ANYMORE. THAT'S WHY IT'S ON SALE.

NO, I DIDN'T SAY THAT. I WAS KIND. I
SUGGESTED SHE BUY THE STUFF, TO WEAR WHEN
SHE'S SINGING WITH VANISH.

MAGGIE SNICKERED. "IF VANISH LASTS."

AMALIA TURNED AWAY AND WANDERED OFF. SHE
DOES NOT LIKE TO TALK ABOUT THAT GROUP
ANYMORE. EVER SINCE JAMES WAS KICKED OUT. HE
IS STILL BOTHERING HER EVERY NOW AND THEN. HE
CALLS AND LEAVES CREEPY MESSAGES ON HER PHONE

MACHINE, THEN ACTS ALL FRIENDLY THE NEXT DAY
AT SCHOOL.

So AMALIA WAS NO HELP EITHER.

GUESS WHO SAVED THE DAY?

THE DUCKMAN.

YES, A GUY WHO LIKES SHOPPING.

DUCKY IS FULL OF HIDDEN TALENTS.

AT FIRST HE WASN'T TOO PROMISING. HE
ACTED EMBARRASSED TO BE IN JUNIORS. HE KEPT
MAKING JOKES AND SAYING HE WAS GOING TO HANG
OUT IN AUTOMOTIVE PARTS.

BUT SOON HE WAS FLIPPING THROUGH THOSE
RACKS. HE FOUND THIS INCREDIBLY COOL COMBO —
SHORT COTTON SKIRT, STRIPED SPANDEX LEGGINGS,
FRINGED MATCHING JACKET . . .

ME.

TOTALLY.

MY BEST GIRLFRIENDS, WHO KNOW ME BETTER
THAN ANYONE IN THE WORLD? CLUELESS COMPARED
TO A HIGH SCHOOL SOPHOMORE GUY I JUST MET
THIS YEAR.

GO FIGURE.

IT'S ALMOST LIKE HE CLIMBS INSIDE MY BRAIN.

I DON'T KNOW WHY I DON'T JUST GO OUT
WITH HIM.

YES, I DO. IT WOULD RUIN THE FRIENDSHIP.

BESIDES, DUCKY'S NOT MY TYPE. FOR A
BOYFRIEND.

BROCK, HOWEVER, IS.

AND WHEN HE SEES THIS OUTFIT, HE IS MINE.

FRIDAY FRIDAY FRIDAY

WHAT AM I DOING IN SCHOOL?

I CAN'T CONCENTRATE!

YES, I CAN.

WHENEVER I SEE BROCK.

AND HE SEES ME. AND SMILES.

AND THE WHOLE SCHOOL IS UTTERLY, TOTALLY,
COMPLETELY,

STARK

RAVING

JEALOUS.

WELL, ALL I CAN SAY TO THAT IS —

POOR EVERYBODY ELSE.

11:45

ᴍᴍᴍᴍᴍᴍᴍᴍᴍᴍᴍᴍᴍᴍᴍᴍᴍᴍᴍᴍᴍᴍᴍ.

SHALL I EXPLAIN THAT LAST ENTRY?

I WILL. IN GREAT DETAIL.

I MAY WANT TO RECAPTURE THIS MOMENT SOMEDAY. WHEN I'M OLDER AND JADED ABOUT MEN. WHEN THE WORLD'S BROCKS ARE FLOCKING AROUND ME.

I'LL ALWAYS REMEMBER HOW IT STARTED.

IT STARTED IN A TRANS AM.

RED.

LOUD.

BRAND-NEW.

WHEN BROCK DROVE UP, DAWN'S MOUTH WAS HANGING OPEN. I SAW IT. SHE WAS STARING OUT HER LIVING ROOM WINDOW.

I NONCHALANTLY WALKED OUT THE FRONT DOOR. STROLLED DOWN THE WALKWAY. SMILED AT BROCK AS HE GOT OUT OF THE CAR. NOT TOO WIDE, NOT TOO GUSHY. JUST ENOUGH TO LEAVE HIM WANTING MORE.

I COULD FEEL THE NEIGHBORHOOD STARING AT US. I COULD FEEL THE HEAT OF THEIR EYES.

BROCK HELD OPEN THE PASSENGER DOOR. HE LOOKED LIKE PERFECTION.

I KISSED HIM ON THE LIPS BEFORE I GOT IN.

He looked kind of shocked. But not unhappy.

Off we went. And Brock said two of the things I wanted to hear the most.

"You look fantastic," and

"You name the restaurant."

I don't know what got into me. Something about the Trans Am made me think of glitz and movie stars and photos in the newspaper gossip columns.

So I said, "Sagebrush Grille." Sort of as a joke.

But Brock didn't take it that way.

He just drove.

When he pulled up to the valet parking of the Grille, right behind a white stretch limo, I was in deep shock. I asked him if he was sure he could afford this.

He said he went there all the time. He said he got into an argument with Brad Pitt there once.

He handed the valet guy a five. He handed the man at the door a ten. He handed the waiter a ten even before he gave us menus. The waiter gave him a funny look.

"To make sure we get good service," Brock whispered to me.

I have no idea what we ate. Some kind of seafood. Brock ordered it for me. I was in a daze.

Who cared about food, anyway? I didn't even eat much of it, because we were talking so much and trying so hard to spot movie stars.

We didn't see any. But that didn't matter either.

After dinner we saw plenty of real stars. In Las Palmas County Park. We happened to run into Brock's friend Pete, who was there with his girlfriend. And Brock seemed happy to see them, so we all hung out. Which meant Brock and I had to behave.

Well, sort of.

I can honestly say that before tonight, I have NOT been kissed.

After Brock, everything else is just touching lips.

And I am about to fall asleep with a big, big smile on my face.

SATURDAY 3/21
11:11 A.M.

I AM SITTING ON MY BED IN DAWN'S ROOM.

I HAVE JUST AWAKENED.

My DIRTY CLOTHES ARE HEAPED AT THE FOOT OF MY BED. ALONG WITH SOME OF MY BOOKS AND TAPES, MY SHOULDER BAG, MY BACKPACK, AND THE GLASS MUG I TOOK FROM THE SAGEBRUSH GRILLE LAST NIGHT.

I DON'T KNOW HOW THEY GOT THERE.

BUT DAWN'S PART OF THE ROOM IS TOTALLY SPOTLESS. EXCEPT FOR ONE CORNER OF HER DRESSER, WHERE MY MAKEUP IS DUMPED INTO A PILE.

I WILL COUNT TO 100.

AND THEN I WILL FIND OUT WHAT HAPPENED.

2:43
PALO CITY BEACH

WELL. DAWN SAYS I'M TOO MESSY. SHE SAYS SHE TRIPPED OVER MY CLOTHES AND TWISTED HER

ANKLE THIS MORNING. SO SHE DUMPED MY STUFF
ON MY BED.

I POLITELY SUGGESTED SHE SHOULD TELL ME
WHENEVER SHE THINKS I'M BEING MESSY, AND I'LL
DO SOMETHING ABOUT IT. BUT I DIDN'T WANT HER
TO THROW MY STUFF AROUND.

WELL, FORGET IT. SHE PUT ON HER LITTLE
HISSY FACE, HER I-WANT-YOU-TO-KNOW-I'M-ANGRY-
BUT-I'M-TOO-CHICKEN-TO-YELL-AT-YOU FACE.

"WHAT?" I SAID. "DIDN'T I SAY THAT NICELY
ENOUGH?"

"I MUST BE MISUNDERSTANDING SOMETHING,"
DAWN REPLIED. "I DIDN'T REALIZE I WAS THE
GUEST AND YOU WERE THE HOST."

I MEAN, PLEASE.

BEFORE I COULD ANSWER, SHE TURNED AWAY
AND STARTED STOMPING OFF.

I GRABBED SOME SHOPPING BAGS. I BARGED
UP INTO THE ROOM, GATHERED MY STUFF INTO THE
BAGS, AND SHOVED THEM IN A CORNER.

"BETTER?" I ASKED.

DAWN WAS SITTING AT HER DESK. "YES," SHE
SAID.

I SMILED SWEETLY. THEN I WENT OUT,
SLAMMING THE DOOR BEHIND ME. I GRABBED A

BEACH TOWEL FROM HOME AND TOOK A BUS
STRAIGHT HERE.

MAYBE I WAS BEING HARSH.

SHE ASKS FOR IT, THOUGH.

8:54 P.M.

HE CAN'T BE MY DAD.

I DO NOT HAVE HIS GENES.

WE ARE FROM TWO DIFFERENT PLANETS.

WE MUST BE.

WHEN HE CAME HOME, HE MUST HAVE NOTICED
MY FOUL MOOD.

COULDN'T HE HAVE ASKED WHAT WAS THE
MATTER?

HE DIDN'T EVEN SAY HELLO!

JUST, "HAVE YOU CALLED YOUR MOTHER
TODAY?"

SO I SAID, "FINE, THANKS, HOW ARE YOU?"

WELL, YOU'D THINK I'D STABBED HIM OR
SOMETHING. HE WAS FURIOUS. "HOW CAN YOU BE SO
DISRESPECTFUL? THE WORSE YOUR MOM GETS, THE
WORSE YOU BEHAVE," BLAH BLAH BLAH. SAME OLD
STORY.

Then he yelled at me for not making dinner. I hadn't even _thought_ about dinner. I ate so much at the beach. And how would I know he hadn't eaten at work?

Then he picked up the phone and began tapping out numbers. "We're calling your mom."

"Now?" I said.

"She's still alive, Sunny. And you mean the world to her, even if you don't care."

HE. SAID. THAT.

I can barely write the words.

He might as well have reached into me and ripped out my heart.

And as I stood there in shock, he waited for Mom to pick up, wearing his best bookstore hello-can-I-help-you smile.

I could hear his words. I could see his lips move. But I couldn't believe what he was saying.

"Hello, sweetheart . . . yes, Sunny and I were just about to sit down to dinner. . . . Fine, fine, it's been a great day. . . . We're all in great spirits. . . . Well, here's your favorite ray of sunshine."

AND THERE IT WAS. THE RECEIVER. RIGHT IN MY FACE.

I TOOK IT AND MUMBLED A HELLO.

MOM SOUNDED ABOUT 80 YEARS OLD. I DESPERATELY WANTED TO SCREAM — TO TELL HER SOMETHING ON MY MIND. BUT I COULDN'T.

I CAN NEVER TELL HER. NOT IN HER STATE. SO I JUST MUMBLED SOME SMALL TALK.

THEN DAD TOOK THE PHONE BACK AND SAID, "HAVE TO CHECK THE STOVE. 'BYE, HONEY."

AS HE HUNG UP, HIS EYES WERE FULL OF TEARS.

HE DIDN'T HEAD FOR THE STOVE AT ALL. INSTEAD, HE DUCKED INTO HIS STUDY, GRABBED SOME PAPERS, AND WENT BACK OUT THE FRONT DOOR. "I'LL GRAB A BITE ON THE ROAD. BE BACK LATE FROM THE STORE, SUNNY. NUKE A FROZEN DINNER FOR YOURSELF, OKAY?"

9:08

I HATE HIM.

THAT'S ALL THERE IS TO IT.

I HATE THE FACT THAT HE LIES TO MOM.

I HATE THE WAY HE TREATS ME AT THE STORE.

I HATE THE WAY HE USES OUR HOUSE AS A CHANGING ROOM.

I HATE FEELING LIKE A SLAVE.

I HATE BEING IGNORED.

AS FAR AS I'M CONCERNED, I DON'T HAVE A DAD.

THIS IS IT.

I AM OUT OF HERE.

FOR GOOD.

10:56

I SHOULD BE HALFWAY TO NEVADA BY NOW.

I TRIED. I WALKED ALL THE WAY TO THE BUS STOP BEFORE I REALIZED I DIDN'T HAVE MY WALLET.

SO I SLIPPED INTO DAWN'S HOUSE TO GET IT.

DAWN WAS TALKING ON THE PHONE TO MAGGIE. SHE BARELY NODDED AS I RACED INTO OUR ROOM.

IF I'D LEFT THROUGH THE FRONT DOOR, I WOULD HAVE MADE IT.

BUT I WENT THROUGH THE BACK. AND I RAN INTO CAROL. SHE WAS AT THE KITCHEN TABLE,

KNITTING SOMETHING THAT LOOKED LIKE AN UGLY
ACRYLIC TUBE SOCK.

SHE ASKED ME WHAT I THOUGHT OF IT.

MY MIND WAS ALREADY OUTSIDE. MY FEET
WERE ITCHING TO GO. I WANTED TO BE MILES
AWAY.

I HAD TO SAY SOMETHING, THOUGH, SO I
ASKED HER IF SHE WAS MAKING IT FOR DAWN.

HER FACE FELL. "IT'S A BABY BOOTIE."

"ARE YOU GIVING BIRTH TO AN ORANGUTAN?"
I SAID.

CAROL PRACTICALLY FELL OFF HER CHAIR
LAUGHING.

IT WASN'T THAT FUNNY. AND I REGRETTED
SAYING IT. IT WAS ONLY PROLONGING THE
CONVERSATION. I DID NOT MEAN TO HANG OUT AND
JOKE AROUND.

BUT IT WAS KIND OF COOL MAKING CAROL
LAUGH.

I LIKE THE WAY SHE LAUGHS.

I THOUGHT ABOUT HOW MUCH I'D MISS HER
WHEN I RAN AWAY. AND HOW MUCH I'D MISS
BEING THERE FOR THE BIRTH.

ALL THE WHILE I WAS STARING AT HER FACE.
IT WAS SO CLEAR. NOT PIMPLE-FREE CLEAR, BUT
JUST PURE HAPPINESS.

And I thought: What a life. How did she get so happy? Was she always like this, even at age 13? Or was she like me?

Then she put her feet up on the next seat. I almost choked when I saw them.

They were ENORMOUS. Like elephant feet.

"Lovely, huh?" she said. "I'm retaining fluid. The baby's making me do it. They really hurt too. And Jack refuses to rub them."

"I will," I said.

Carol gave me a look. "You will?"

I shrugged. "If you want. They're clean, aren't they?"

"Last time I checked."

I pulled over my chair, took her right foot, and began massaging it. The way Mom used to massage mine — and I hers, back when she first got sick.

Back before the rubbing began to hurt her so much.

Carol was sighing and oohing. It reminded me so much of Mom.

Too much.

I had to stop.

Carol dropped her knitting on the table.

She put her feet down and leaned close to me.

"Are you okay?" she asked gently.

A couple of tears started down my cheeks.

I felt like such a fool. I <u>hate</u> crying and I <u>hate</u> people who cry too much.

I was so freaked out, I didn't know what to say. So I said, "I'm sorry" about ten times.

Carol didn't seem to mind. She just sat there, her arm around my shoulder. I could hear the rush of a car passing by. Dawn's chattery voice on the phone. The drone of the TV show that Mr. Schafer and Jeff were watching.

"Anytime you want to talk, just tell me," Carol said softly.

"You don't want to hear," I replied.

"I do, Sunny. I care about you. I know this is a rough time. Please. I'm in no hurry."

I didn't mean to unload. But my thoughts were all bottled up. All the feelings for Mom. All the hate for Dad.

So I told her what had happened over

THE LAST FEW DAYS. RIGHT UP TO MY BIG
ARGUMENT WITH DAD.

I EXPECTED AN ADULT ANSWER. I FIGURED
SHE'D DEFEND DAD, THE WAY ALL ADULTS DEFEND
EACH OTHER.

BUT THE FIRST THING SHE SAID WAS, "THAT'S
NOT FAIR."

"HE'S SUCH A LIAR!" I BLURTED OUT. "HOW
CAN HE DO THAT TO MOM?"

"NO." CAROL SHOOK HER HEAD. "THAT'S NOT
THE IMPORTANT QUESTION. HE WANTS TO SOOTHE
HER, SUNNY. I WOULD DO THE SAME THING. IT'S
YOU HE NEEDS TO THINK ABOUT." SHE RAISED AN
EYEBROW AT ME. "DON'T YOU EVER TELL YOUR DAD
I SAID THAT."

I TOLD HER I DIDN'T TELL HIM ANYTHING
ANYWAY. I PROMISED NOT TO START.

"I DON'T QUITE KNOW HOW TO SAY THIS,"
CAROL WENT ON. "WHAT YOUR DAD'S FACING IS A
LITTLE LIKE WHAT JACK FACED WHEN HE DIVORCED
DAWN'S MOTHER."

"MY MOM IS NOT —"

"I KNOW. I KNOW. BUT WHAT I MEAN IS, HIS
REALITY IS CHANGING, SUNNY. AND SO'S YOURS.
IT'S SCARY. YOU FEEL LIKE YOUR LIFE IS SPINNING
OUT OF CONTROL. WELL, YOUR DAD FEELS THAT

too. You don't know what 'normal' is anymore. He doesn't either. It's up to both of you to define it again. But it's going to take a long time. And a lot of work."

"Normal? How can we ever be normal, Carol? When Mom's in the hospital and Dad's in the store, and I'm over here all the time, freeloading off you."

Carol smiled and gave me a big hug. "No, you're not freeloading. We love having you. And don't worry, sweetie. This won't last forever. You'll see. It'll never be the same as it was, but it'll be good again. Just give it time."

Dawn is so lucky.

Carol is the coolest.

I have been thinking of her words ever since we talked.

I guess she's right. I want her to be right.

But I can't imagine how she could be.

I try hard to picture a normal life. With Dad. After you-know-what.

But it's impossible.

Dad won't have to work less. I'll still never see him.

HE WON'T CLONE HIMSELF EITHER. THE HOUSE
WILL BE EMPTY EVERY DAY WHEN I COME HOME.
   AND WHEN I AM WITH HIM, THEN WHAT? WILL
HE CHANGE? WILL HE EVER THINK ABOUT MY
FEELINGS, OR AT LEAST STOP TREATING ME LIKE
I'M A STRANGER?
   NORMAL.
   WHAT DOES THAT MEAN, ANYWAY?
   ANOTHER WIFE FOR DAD? A STEPMOTHER?
   GREAT. I'LL HAVE TO SEE HIM HOLDING HANDS
WITH A STRANGE WOMAN AROUND THE HOUSE. I'LL
HAVE TO MAKE THEM MEALS.
   I HATE HER ALREADY.
   WELL, UNLESS SHE'S LIKE CAROL.
   HA.
   KNOWING DAD, SHE WON'T EVEN BE CLOSE.

MONDAY 3/23
SCIENCE

   I CANNOT BELIEVE THIS.
   THIS IS NOT HAPPENING TO ME.
   PETE ASKED ME OUT.
   PETE, BROCK'S FRIEND.
   AND I SAID YES.

WHO DO I THINK I AM?

I'M INSANE.

No, I'M NOT.

I'M A FREE PERSON.

I AM NOT MARRIED TO BROCK. HOW DO I KNOW HE'S NOT SEEING OTHER GIRLS?

BESIDES, I GOT A GOOD LOOK AT PETE TODAY. ACTUALLY, A COUPLE OF GOOD LOOKS.

HE'S CUTER THAN BROCK.

DAWN IS SHOCKED.

DAWN THINKS THE WORLD IS COMING TO AN END BECAUSE I WANT TO GO OUT WITH PETE NELSON.

Dawn thinks I should "talk this out" with Brock.

Dawn also thinks I should have talked out Brock with Chris.

Dawn really needs to grow up.

But I can't tell her that.

Why?

Because. Dawn. Is. My. Best. Friend.

Tuesday 3/24
2:45 p.m.

Home early today.

I could not face the last couple of periods.

Not in my frame of mind.

It's all because of Ducky.

He was a total wreck this morning. He came to school crying.

He wouldn't admit it, but he did. His eyes were all raw and watery.

He definitely needed someone to talk to.

He's been there for me so often. The least I could do was return the favor.

Well, I tried. But he kept changing the

CONVERSATION — "HOW ARE _you_ DOING? OH, I ALMOST FORGOT TO ASK. ARE YOU STILL MAD AT YOUR DAD?"

DUCKY "YOU FIRST" MCCRAE.

I WAS NOT GOING TO LET HIM OFF EASY. I HAD TO FIND OUT WHAT HAD HAPPENED. SO I CUT MATH AND YANKED HIM OUT OF THE CAFETERIA DURING 10TH-GRADE LUNCH.

I WANTED TO DRAG HIM TO THE FIESTA GRILL. HE'S ALLOWED TO GO THERE DURING LUNCH. BUT HE KEPT REMINDING ME THAT 8TH-GRADERS ARE _NOT_ ALLOWED AND _I_ WOULD GET INTO TROUBLE. LIKE I CARE.

SO WE WENT OUTSIDE AND HID IN THE BACKSEAT OF HIS CAR. WHICH SMELLS TERRIBLE. AND IS CRAMPED. AND HAS GUM IN THE CARPET.

(I AM _SUCH_ A GOOD FRIEND.)

DUCKY'S PROBLEM?

ALEX.

ALEX THE DRIP.

ALEX, WHO DOESN'T DESERVE TO _LOOK_ AT DUCKY.

HERE'S WHAT HAPPENED: DUCKY HAD GONE TO PICK HIM UP THIS MORNING, AND ALEX HAD YELLED AT HIM AND TOLD HIM TO GO AWAY.

YES, THAT WAS IT.

I NEARLY SMACKED DUCKY.

"DON'T WASTE TIME WITH PEOPLE WHO TAKE ADVANTAGE OF YOU," I TOLD DUCKY.

I SHOULD KNOW.

"HE'S A GOOD GUY," DUCKY INSISTED. "JUST SERIOUSLY DEPRESSED. HE'S BEEN CUTTING SCHOOL. DISAPPEARING WITHOUT LETTING HIS MOM KNOW WHERE HE IS. ACTING HOSTILE TO EVERYONE —"

"SOUNDS LIKE ME," I SAID.

"SOMETIMES I WORRY ABOUT YOU TOO," DUCKY REPLIED. "BUT I KNOW YOU, SUNNY. YOU'RE THERE. WITH A HEART AND A SOUL. ALEX IS LOST. YOU'RE NOT."

"OH, REALLY?" I SAID.

"I MEAN, YOU CONNECT. LIKE NOW. LOOK, I KNOW WHAT YOU'RE GOING THROUGH. I KNOW IT'S REALLY HARD. BUT YOU'LL COME OUT THE OTHER END, SUNNY. BECAUSE YOU'RE NOT SHUTTING DOWN. YOU NEVER WILL." DUCKY GRINNED. "I WON'T LET YOU."

COOL, OR WHAT?

HE JUST GIVES AND GIVES AND GIVES. AND HE NEVER SEEMS TO WANT ANYTHING IN RETURN.

I WISH ALL MY FRIENDS WERE LIKE THAT.

5:15 P.M.

I DID IT.

I FIGURED OUT A WAY TO GIVE BACK TO Ducky.

A JOB.

DAD NEEDS A CLERK. SOMEONE OLD ENOUGH TO WORK PART-TIME, LEGALLY. SOMEONE WHO IS NOT ME.

Ducky NEEDS THE MONEY. HIS PARENTS ARE IN GHANA, AND HIS OLDER BROTHER IS _ALWAYS_ BORROWING CASH FROM HIM AND NOT PAYING IT BACK.

I MEAN, DUH. WHY HADN'T I THOUGHT OF THIS BEFORE?

I JUST CALLED TO TELL HIM MY IDEA.

HE LOVED IT. HE PROMISED HE'D APPLY.

I'LL PUT IN A GOOD WORD FOR HIM.

ACTUALLY, MAYBE I WON'T.

KNOWING DAD, HE'LL REFUSE TO HIRE HIM FOR THAT REASON ALONE.

WEDNESDAY 3/25
8:25 A.M.

"DOES THIS YOUNG DUCKY FELLOW HAVE ANY REFERENCES? IS HE LITERATE? DOES HE PRESENT A CLEAN APPEARANCE?"

WHAT KIND OF STUPID QUESTIONS ARE THOSE?

UH, NO, DAD. HE WEARS DREDS, HAS A PIERCED TONGUE, CAN'T READ, AND LIKES TO PICK HIS NOSE IN FRONT OF CUSTOMERS.

I SHOULD NEVER HAVE TALKED TO HIM.

I SHOULD HAVE RUN OFF WHEN I HAD THE CHANCE.

AND NOW LOOK WHAT I'M DOING.

INFLICTING HIM ON DUCKY.

STUDY HALL

I FLUNKED YESTERDAY'S MATH QUIZ.

THE REASON: I DIDN'T TAKE YESTERDAY'S MATH QUIZ.

BECAUSE I WAS OUT OF CLASS, AND BECAUSE I DIDN'T HAVE A NOTE, AND BECAUSE MS. WHALEN IS A CRUEL AND HEARTLESS EXCUSE FOR A HUMAN BEING, I GOT AN AUTOMATIC F.

She told me this while I was leaving class today. Then she gave me this look, like I was supposed to kiss her feet and say I'm sorry.

Puh-leeze. I just shrugged.

"Don't you care?" she asked.

I shrugged again.

I love seeing the Whale fume.

She started yelling at me, but I left in the middle of it.

Dawn was waiting for me in the hallway.

"Why did you do that?" she asked.

"Do what, flunk?" I said. "She didn't even give me a chance."

"You cut the quiz, Sunny!"

"I didn't know there was a quiz."

"That's not a good excuse!"

"Okay, when I think of a better one, I'll tell you."

Dawn threw her hands up and walked away. "See you later, Sunny."

That's what she thinks.

4:14 P.M.

AM RIDING TO THE VISTA HILLS MALL.
CAROL'S DRIVING.

DON'T KNOW WHERE DAWN IS.

SHE'S PROBABLY WITH THE WHALE AS WE SPEAK.
TALKING ABOUT WAYS TO MAKE MY LIFE MORE
PAINFUL.

WHICH IS WHY I WALKED HOME ALONE. AND
WHY CAROL INVITED ME — WITHOUT DAWN — TO KEEP
HER COMPANY WHILE SHE SHOPS.

NICE TO KNOW SOMEONE CARES.

SO I AM GOING MATERNITY SHOPPING.

AND I'M HAPPY ABOUT IT.

ME.

WHO'D HAVE EVER THOUGHT?

4:34

BOB.

BILL.

BRUCE.

WHAT'S HIS NAME?

BLONDISH-BROWN HAIR. CURLY. SQUARE JAW.
GREAT SHOULDERS.

I'VE SEEN HIM IN SCHOOL A MILLION TIMES OUT
OF THE CORNER OF MY EYE.

I SHOULD HAVE LOOKED CLOSER.

OKAY, HE'S JUST PAST THE DRESSING ROOMS.
IN THE HOUSEWARES SECTION. WHO'S HE WITH?
PROBABLY SOME INCREDIBLE-LOOKING JUNIOR
GIRLFRIEND.

NO.

SHE'S OLD.

HIS MOM!

IT MUST BE.

THERE'S HOPE.

CAN'T LET HIM SEE ME IN MATERNITY. THAT IS
DEFINITELY THE WRONG IMPRESSION.

I'LL STROLL AROUND. I'LL PRETEND I'M
LOOKING FOR A BLENDER.

CAROL IS TAKING FOREVER IN THAT
DRESSING ROOM. I WONDER IF SHE'D MIND IF I

5:24

AT THE HOSPITAL

I CAN BARELY THINK.

MY FINGERS ARE TIRED.

MY BODY IS TIRED. I NEED SLEEP.

But I feel TERRIBLE. I feel like it's all my fault.

I have to write this out.

Everything happened so fast.

I was such a fool. Sitting there, bored, worrying about what's-his-name — Bo Something.

Did it even occur to me why Carol might be taking so long?

Maybe if I hadn't been so distracted, I would have called to her and asked how she was doing. Maybe I would have heard her fall to the dressing room floor.

Well, someone did. Some little old lady who began to shriek.

I could see Carol's hand sticking out from underneath the dressing room door. I tried to pull the door open, but it was locked. I yelled for help.

The shrieking lady was sitting in a chair. Three people were helping her.

But no one was helping me. A couple of shoppers were gawking, still holding their purchases. Like I was a TV screen.

Finally I ran out and found a clerk.

The two of us crawled under the door.

Carol was almost out. Eyes flickering. Slumped on the floor.

"Are you okay?" I asked.

"I feel faint." She was barely forming the words. Her voice was tiny.

"Is it the baby?" I yelled. "Is it coming?"

Carol shook her head. "I don't think so."

"Don't just stand there," I said to the clerk. "Get some help."

The clerk looked horrified. "The manager's on break," she said.

Useless.

I ran out and made the nearest cashier call 911 for me on the store phone. I grabbed the receiver and told the operator what had happened.

When I ran back, I had to elbow through a crowd. I heard someone say, "There's the daughter."

I glanced around looking for Dawn, until I realized the person was talking about _me_.

Carol was sitting up now, her back against the dressing room wall. She looked bone-white. The clerk was squatting by her side, holding her hand.

I KNELT DOWN AND PUT MY ARM AROUND CAROL. I ASKED THE CLERK TO GET HER A GLASS OF WATER. I PRACTICALLY BARKED AT THE CROWD, TELLING THEM TO MAKE ROOM. IT WAS INCREDIBLY STUFFY.

"I FEEL WEAK," CAROL SAID. "I DON'T KNOW WHAT'S HAPPENING TO ME."

"YOU'LL BE OKAY," I SAID.

"I'M SCARED, SUNNY."

I WASN'T. THAT'S THE WEIRD THING. I WAS THINKING ABOUT WHAT HAD TO BE DONE. IN ORDER OF IMPORTANCE.

1. STAY WITH CAROL WHILE WE WAIT.
2. MAKE SURE SHE GETS TO THE HOSPITAL.
3. CALL MR. SCHAFER AT WORK.
4. CALL MRS. BRUEN AT HOME.

THE PLACE WAS SWARMING NOW. CUSTOMERS, CLERKS, SECURITY GUARDS, CRACKLING RADIOS. POOR CAROL. LIKE SHE REALLY NEEDED ALL THIS.

I DIDN'T MOVE FROM CAROL'S SIDE (STEP 1). I FED HER SIPS OF WATER. I BORROWED A CELL PHONE FROM ONE OF THE GAWKERS AND DID STEPS 3 AND 4.

IT FELT LIKE WE WERE THERE FOR HOURS. I WAS SO RELIEVED WHEN THE EMS CREW SHOWED UP.

They put Carol on a stretcher and carried her to a service elevator.

I rode down with them, then followed them out a back entrance, where the ambulance was waiting.

One technician asked if I was "kin." Carol quickly answered yes. I guess she figured they wouldn't let me ride with her if I wasn't kin. I hopped into the back and held Carol's hand as we sped toward the hospital.

Daughter for a day.

Fine with me. More than fine. I was proud.

On the way, the technicians hooked Carol up to a couple of IVs. One of them took her pulse.

"Am I going to lose my baby?" Carol asked.

"This kind of thing isn't abnormal," the technician said. "Pregnancy is complicated."

"That wasn't the question," I reminded him.

The technician nodded and smiled. "The baby's probably going to be just fine."

Probably.

I never thought that word could be so scary.

WHAT DOES IT MEAN? 95 PERCENT? 51 PERCENT?

I WANT TO ASK THE DOCTOR, BUT I CAN'T. I'M IN THE PALO CITY HOSPITAL EMERGENCY ROOM WAITING AREA NOW, WHICH IS ABOUT THE MOST DEPRESSING PLACE IN THE WORLD, BESIDES HOME. CAROL'S IN ROOM 209, BEING EXAMINED.

I HAVE NO IDEA WHAT'S HAPPENING IN THERE.

THE TV IS BLARING A SOCCER GAME IN SPANISH. TO MY RIGHT, A LITTLE KID IS SNEEZING AND COUGHING AND CRYING. ACROSS THE ROOM, A YOUNG GUY IS ALL BANDAGED UP. TO MY LEFT, AN OLD MAN IS SLUMPED IN A CHAIR, ASLEEP.

AT LEAST I HOPE HE'S ASLEEP.

I AM TOTALLY, TOTALLY FREAKED OUT.

11:12 P.M.

HOME NOW.

WELL, AT DAWN'S.

I CAN'T BELIEVE HOW LATE IT IS.

THIS DAY FEELS LIKE IT LASTED A MONTH.

LUCKILY I WASN'T ALONE TOO LONG IN THE WAITING ROOM. MR. SCHAFER CAME BARGING IN AS I WAS WRITING.

He was pale and anxious. He looked like he'd aged about 10 years.

I told him where Carol was, and he ran right in to see her.

The receptionist wasn't too happy about that, but he ignored her. So did I. I followed him.

The door to Room 209 was open, and a doctor was chatting with Carol. His name tag said Dr. C. Rymond.

Carol was still hooked to IVs, but she looked a lot better.

Mr. Schafer threw his arms around her. They both started crying.

"We're f-f-f-fine!" Carol blurted out.

"Mama and baby both pulled through with flying colors," Dr. Rymond agreed. "That's the good news."

Mr. Schafer turned warily. "Is there **bad** news?"

Dr. Rymond smiled. "If you consider total rest and relaxation bad news. I'm prescribing confinement to bed until the baby is born. No getting up at all."

"But that's TWO MONTHS!" Mr. Schafer replied.

Dr. Rymond explained that she'd better do what he said if she wanted to keep the baby. Well, he didn't use those exact words, but that was the meaning.

Mr. Schafer clasped Carol's hand and asked how she felt about this.

She smiled. She said she would finally have time to read all her magazines. "Besides," she went on, "I love meals in bed and long foot rubs."

She winked at me. I winked back.

God, I hope I'm like her when I grow up.

A few moments later Dr. Rymond said he had to do a few more tests and he needed to be alone with Carol.

I told them I'd wait outside. Mr. Schafer told Carol he'd be right back, and he walked out with me.

"Thanks," he said. "I don't know what would have happened if you weren't there. You saved her, Sunny. You saved both of their lives."

"Both?" I said.

"Carol's," he replied, "and the baby's."

Saved their lives.

I hadn't thought of it that way.

I had been so busy DOING, I hadn't really been THINKING.

But imagine if I hadn't been there at all. Would someone have seen Carol and called 911 in time? Maybe not. Then what? She might have fallen unconscious. Become dehydrated. Or worse.

But she didn't.

Because of me.

Me, Sunny the Useless, Ungrateful Daughter.

I felt about ten feet tall.

"I'll wait here," Mr. Schafer said. "And I'll drive you home. If you want to go visit your mom, feel free. I won't leave without you. In fact, I'd like to say hi too. I'll meet you in her room, okay?"

Actually, I hadn't thought of visiting Mom.

Not that I didn't WANT to. But at that moment, I was sort of connected to Carol. I didn't feel like leaving her just yet, after all we'd been through.

I told him I didn't mind waiting. But he gave me a funny look. Like, you DON'T want to visit your own mother?

So I started to leave.

I met Dawn, Jeff, and Mrs. Bruen in the hallway.

They started firing questions at me. Jeff asked if Carol was dead. Dawn was worried about the baby. Both of them were crying. Mrs. Bruen was busy trying to keep them from blocking the hallway.

I held Jeff's and Dawn's hands. I calmed them down and told them everything was all right. I brought them into the waiting room.

While Mr. Schafer gave them the details, I headed for the cancer wing.

Mom was sleeping, but she woke up when I walked in.

"Robin," she said. "Hi."

Robin?

"It's Sunny, Mom," I reminded her.

Then I realized who she meant. My aunt. Mom's little sister, who died shortly after I was born.

Mom blinked. Then she laughed weakly. She said she'd been having a dream. Her brother, sisters, and all her cousins were gathered around her. They were little children, but they were strong enough to lift her in the air,

UPWARD AND UPWARD UNTIL THEIR HEADS WERE IN THE CLOUDS.

I SAT. I LISTENED. I TRIED TO CHAT, BUT MOM WAS IN HER OWN DREAMY WORLD.

WHEN MR. SCHAFER FINALLY CAME IN, DAWN AND JEFF WERE WITH HIM. DAWN HAD A BOUQUET OF FLOWERS. SHE PUT THEM ON THE NIGHT TABLE, GAVE MOM A BIG KISS, AND FUSSED ABOUT HOW GREAT MOM LOOKED.

THAT WAS DAWN'S WORD OF THE DAY. GREAT. "DOESN'T SHE LOOK GREAT? YOU LOOK SO GREAT!"

AND ALL I COULD THINK WAS:

I HADN'T COMPLIMENTED MOM.

I HADN'T BROUGHT HER FLOWERS.

I HADN'T EVEN KISSED HER.

AND THE TRUTH WAS, SHE DIDN'T LOOK GREAT. SHE LOOKED WITHERED AND SICK AND GROGGY.

BUT DAWN JUST PLOPPED HERSELF IN FRONT OF ME, GUSHING AWAY. LYING.

AND BLOCKING ME FROM MOM.

EXCUSE ME. I'M ONLY HER DAUGHTER.

DAWN WAS IN HIGH MOTORMOUTH MODE. WHEN SHE FINISHED COMPLIMENTING MOM AND GUSHING ABOUT HER OWN FLOWERS, SHE TOLD MOM ABOUT CAROL'S ACCIDENT.

FINALLY MOM LOOKED ALERT. "OH, MY

GOODNESS," SHE SAID. "SUNNY HASN'T MENTIONED THIS."

"I WAS ABOUT TO," I SAID.

BUT I COULDN'T GET A WORD IN EDGEWISE, I DIDN'T SAY. BECAUSE DAWN WAS TALKING ENOUGH FOR ABOUT FIFTEEN PEOPLE.

AND SHE KEPT ON, WHILE JEFF WANDERED AROUND AND MR. SCHAFER CHASED AFTER HIM AND I DID MY IMPRESSION OF A BARCALOUNGER.

THE NEXT THING I KNEW, MR. SCHAFER WAS READY TO TAKE US HOME. I MANAGED A QUICK GOOD-BYE TO MOM.

DURING THE CAR RIDE, DAWN FINALLY SHUT UP. WE ALL DID. WE WERE EXHAUSTED.

BACK AT THE SCHAFERS', EVERYONE GRUNTED GOOD NIGHT AND WENT OFF TO BED. EXCEPT MR. SCHAFER. HE WENT BACK TO THE HOSPITAL.

I SHOULD BE FAST ASLEEP, BUT I CAN'T STOP THINKING ABOUT CAROL.

SHE COMES HOME TOMORROW. I WON'T FEEL TOTALLY COMFORTABLE UNTIL THEN.

DAWN OBVIOUSLY FEELS FINE. SHE'S IN BED, SNOOZING LIKE A CONTENTED SHEEP.

I THINK I'LL SPEND THE NIGHT RIGHT HERE, ON THE SCHAFERS' SOFA.

I FEEL LIKE BEING ALONE.

WOKE UP LATE THIS MORNING. DAWN WAS
ALREADY LEAVING FOR SCHOOL. I TOLD HER I'D
MEET HER THERE.

I DIDN'T.

I WENT HOME FOR A CHANGE OF CLOTHES.

DAD WAS EATING BREAKFAST. I TOLD HIM
WHAT HAPPENED TO CAROL. HE HALF LISTENED WHILE
HE WAS READING THE PAPER.

"THAT'S TOUGH," WAS HIS ANALYSIS OF THE
SITUATION.

END OF DISCUSSION.

THANK YOU FOR YOUR SUPPORT, DAD.

WHY IS HE LIKE THIS?

HE DIDN'T USED TO BE. WE HAD FUN WHEN I
WAS A KID.

OR MAYBE MY MEMORY IS PLAYING TRICKS.
MAYBE HE WAS ALWAYS UNBEARABLE, ONLY I DIDN'T
RECOGNIZE IT.

I TURNED TO GO UPSTAIRS.

"I'M MEETING THAT BOY TODAY," DAD CALLED
AFTER ME. "CHRISTOPHER. QUACKY. WHATEVER YOU
CALL HIM."

"DUCKY," I SAID.

"HE SOUNDS LIKE A NICE BOY ON THE PHONE.
LET'S JUST HOPE HE CAN ALPHABETIZE."
THAT WAS SUPPOSED TO BE A JOKE, I THINK.
I DIDN'T EVEN SMILE.

                                                    7:54

        I HELPED BRING CAROL BACK FROM THE
HOSPITAL. SHE WAS SO GRATEFUL TO ME. SHE SAID
SHE WOULD FEEL SAFE IN ANY EMERGENCY WITH ME.
SHE SAID I HAD THE QUICK WITS OF SOMEONE
TWICE MY AGE.
        EVERYONE (EXCEPT DAWN) WAS MAKING A BIG
FUSS.
        I LOVED IT.
        I INSISTED ON ROLLING CAROL TO HER ROOM
IN HER WHEELCHAIR. MR. SCHAFER, MRS. BRUEN,
AND I EASED HER INTO BED.
        THEN WE ALL CELEBRATED WITH TAKE-OUT THAI
FOOD ON PORTABLE TRAYS IN HER ROOM.
        DAWN DIDN'T SAY MUCH.
        I THINK SHE'S JEALOUS.

HE FOUND MY LOCKER.

BEFORE HOMEROOM.

HE HAD TO WALK ALL THE WAY ACROSS SCHOOL.

AND HE DID IT JUST TO PUT HIS ARMS AROUND ME FROM BEHIND AND WHISPER IN MY EAR, "ARE WE STILL ON FOR TONIGHT?"

DOES HE <u>KNOW</u> HOW THAT MAKES ME FEEL?

HE MUST.

HE'S A JUNIOR.

I WAS COOL. I DID NOT ACT SHOCKED. I DID NOT ANSWER HIM LIKE A 13-YEAR-OLD.

I JUST SMILED AT HIM AND TOUCHED HIS HAND. AS IF THIS KIND OF THING HAPPENED TO ME EVERY DAY.

AND I SAID, "I'M ON IF YOU ARE, PETE."

DAWN WAS STARING <u>FIERCELY</u> INTO HER LOCKER. I KNOW SHE WANTED TO GIVE ME ONE OF HER TSK-TSK LOOKS.

TOO BAD.

I GAVE PETE A KISS, PUT MY ARM IN HIS, AND WALKED WITH HIM DOWN THE HALLWAY. SLOWLY.

SO DAWN COULD WATCH OUR EVERY STEP.

I LOVE HIS VOICE.

I LOVE HIS COLOGNE.

I LOVE THE FEEL OF HIS ARM AROUND MY WAIST.

PETE NELSON, WHERE HAVE YOU BEEN MY WHOLE LIFE?

I WISH WE COULD GET AN EARLY START. CUT SCHOOL RIGHT NOW AND PARTY UNTIL MIDNIGHT. JUST THE TWO OF US.

OH, WELL. I'LL HAVE TO WAIT UNTIL LATER.

DETAILS AT 11.

BUT DON'T HOLD ME TO IT.

SATURDAY MORNING

OKAY, DETAILS AT 12:31 (A.M., THAT IS).

PETE COULDN'T BELIEVE HOW LATE I WAS "ALLOWED" TO STAY UP. THAT'S THE WAY HE PUT IT. ALLOWED. LIKE I WAS A LITTLE KID.

I TOLD HIM I MAKE THE RULES IN MY HOUSE.

I TOLD HIM I HAVE UNLIMITED FREEDOM.

HE WAS IMPRESSED.

OKAY, THE VERDICT. ON A SCALE FROM 1 TO 10, BORING TO ABSOLUTELY FAB.

THE MOVIE: 3 FOR THE FILM, 10 FOR THE WAY WE IGNORED IT, WHICH LEADS TO

KISSING TECHNIQUE: A DEFINITE 11. MAKES

WHAT'S-HIS-FACE FROM LAST WEEK LOOK LIKE MICKEY MOUSE.

FACE FACTOR: 8-. GREAT CHEEKBONES. SOME PIMPLES AT EYE LEVEL.

POST-MOVIE: 7. OKAY, PIZZA'S FINE. AND PETE DOES WORK PART-TIME AT PIZZA PARADISE, SO IT MADE SENSE TO GO THERE. BUT AFTER YOU'VE BEEN TO THE SAGEBRUSH GRILLE, NOTHING IS EVER THE SAME.

CONVERSATION: WHO CARES?

GENERAL IMPACT: 9+. POSSIBILITY FOR IMPROVEMENT IN THE RESTAURANT AREA, BUT OTHERWISE PERFECTION.

ASSESSMENT FOR FUTURE: A KEEPER.

SATURDAY
10:59 A.M.

OH. FORGOT TO MENTION.

WHEN I GOT HOME LAST NIGHT, I FOUND A MESSAGE FROM CHRIS ON THE PHONE MACHINE.

CHRIS THE BASKETBALL FAN.

HE ASKED ME OUT FOR NEXT WEEKEND.

UH-HUH.

DREAM ON.

8:02 P.M.

I CANNOT BELIEVE DAWN.

WHO DOES SHE THINK SHE IS?

SHE SHOWS UP AT 6:15. SHE WALKS INTO HER KITCHEN WHILE I'M SLAVING OVER DINNER. AND INSTEAD OF SAYING THANKS, WHICH SHE SHOULD DO, SHE YELLS AT ME:

"WHO TOLD YOU TO MAKE DINNER? WHO CHANGED THE SCHEDULE? IT'S NOT YOUR TURN, SUNNY, IT'S MINE!"

I NEARLY THREW THE CAESAR SALAD (WITH CHICKEN) AT HER. I SAID, EXCUSE ME, BUT THIS IS NOT THE ARMY. AND IT IS DINNERTIME. CAROL IS IN HER ROOM, HUNGRY AND UNABLE TO TAKE CARE OF HERSELF. THE MEAL NEEDED TO BE MADE.

BUT THAT WASN'T ENOUGH FOR JULIA CHILD. SHE HAD BOUGHT FILLETS OF FLOUNDER. AND THEY HAD TO BE EATEN TONIGHT. NOW THEY WERE GOING TO SPOIL.

I WANTED TO TAKE THE FISH AND WHAP HER UPSIDE THE HEAD WITH IT.

THEN CAROL CALLED, AND WE BOTH RAN TO HER ROOM.

GOOD OLD CAROL. SHE THANKED DAWN FOR THE FISH AND ASSURED HER THAT IT WOULD TASTE

FINE TOMORROW. SHE EXPLAINED THAT I WAS JUST TRYING TO HELP DAWN OUT. SHE SAID SHE HAD THOUGHT DAWN WOULD BE <u>HAPPY</u> TO BE RELIEVED OF DINNER DUTY.

UH-HUH. SURE. DAWN GRUMBLED ALL THROUGH DINNER AND EXCUSED HERSELF EARLY.

IT'S JEALOUSY. HAS TO BE. GROW UP, DAWN.

ANYWAY, JEFF WASN'T MUCH BETTER AT THE DINNER TABLE, AND HE HAD NO EXCUSE. HE TOOK ONE LOOK AT MY BEAUTIFUL SALAD AND SAID, "CAN I HAVE A PEANUT BUTTER SANDWICH?"

SO I HAD A COZY, INTIMATE DINNER, EATING OFF MY LITTLE PORTABLE TABLE IN THE MASTER BEDROOM, ALONG WITH CAROL AND MR. SCHAFER. THE TWO <u>MATURE</u> MEMBERS OF THE FAMILY.

SUNDAY 3/29
11:05 P.M.

A FEW IMPORTANT ITEMS.

NUMBER ONE. THE SCHAFERS ARE THE FAMILY I SHOULD HAVE HAD.

I FEEL SO <u>WELCOME</u> IN THEIR HOUSE. DESPITE DAWN.

IN THEIR HOUSE I AM NOT ROBO SLAVE DAUGHTER. I'M ALLOWED TO BE A PERSON. A HERO, REALLY. MR. SCHAFER AND CAROL JUST CAN'T STOP THANKING ME FOR WHAT I DID.

I CAN'T BELIEVE I ACTUALLY USED TO RESENT CAROL. I NEVER WANTED TO TALK TO HER. I GUESS I WAS SIDING WITH DAWN. BUT THAT SEEMS LIKE AGES AGO.

DAWN SHOULD REALIZE HOW LUCKY SHE IS.

NUMBER TWO. DUCKY HAS A JOB AT WINSLOW BOOKS.

HE CALLED ME AT DAWN'S. HE WAS PRACTICALLY SCREAMING WITH HAPPINESS.

ABOUT WORKING WITH DAD.

I BEHAVED. I DID NOT BURST HIS BUBBLE.

DAD GAVE HIM THE JOB TODAY. (DID DAD TELL ME? OF COURSE NOT.) DUCKY STARTS TUESDAY AFTER SCHOOL.

TO CELEBRATE, HE INSISTED ON TAKING ME OUT FOR DESSERT.

NOW, IF I HAD BEEN AT MY HOME, DAD WOULD HAVE SAID NO. HE'D HAVE FOUND SOME STUPID CHORE FOR ME TO DO AROUND THE

HOUSE. SOMETHING HE'S TOO LAZY TO DO
HIMSELF.

    BUT MR. SCHAFER DIDN'T EVEN BLINK. NO
WARNINGS, NO CURFEW, NOTHING. HE JUST SAID,
"HAVE FUN."

    SO I GRABBED MY BIKE AND WENT TO A HOT
SPOT THAT DUCKY AND I HAD AGREED ON.

    PIZZA PARADISE — HOME, STRANGELY ENOUGH,
OF PALO CITY'S BEST SUNDAES.

    NUMBER THREE. PETE DOESN'T WORK THERE ON
SUNDAY NIGHTS.

    NUMBER FOUR. BUT BO <u>ROLLINS</u> DOES. THAT'S
HIS FULL NAME. I FOUND OUT. HOW? DUCKY TOLD
ME. WHICH LEADS ME TO

    NUMBER FIVE. FOR A GUY, DUCKY IS A GREAT
GOSSIP.

    NOT THAT GIRLS ARE THE <u>ONLY</u> GOSSIPS.
PERSONALLY, I BELIEVE GUYS ARE EVEN WORSE.
THEY JUST LIKE TO PRETEND THEY AREN'T.

    DUCKY'S DIFFERENT. HE DISHES DIRECTLY. I LIKE
THAT.

When I arrived at Pizza Paradise, I spotted his car parked down the block, in front of the convenience store. Ducky emerged with a bag full of groceries. Chips, pretzels, and candy, along with some toilet paper and drain cleaner.

"Groceries for me and Ted," he explained.

I helped him load the trunk. As we walked inside Pizza Paradise, I told Ducky I envied him. I mean, what a cool life, living alone with his big brother. Sometimes I wish Dad were a traveling professor like Ducky's dad. Then he'd have to spend most of the year in places like Ghana too. My life would be so much easier.

Ducky made a face. He said his brother is a pig. Ted never buys food or does laundry or cleans.

Which, to me, doesn't seem like a big deal. I mean, Dad doesn't do any of that stuff either. Whenever it has to be done, he just yells at me to do it.

"Believe me," Ducky said, sliding into a booth at the back of the restaurant, "you would not want to be in my shoes."

I could feel Ducky tensing up, so I

BACKED OFF. OUR ONE AND ONLY ARGUMENT HAD
STARTED THIS WAY. I DIDN'T WANT A NUMBER TWO.

So I ASKED ABOUT THE JOB.

DUCKY'S FACE LIT UP. HE TOLD ME THAT DAD
WAS PERFECTLY NICE TO HIM AT THE INTERVIEW. HE
SAID DAD EVEN CRACKED A FEW GOOD JOKES. (I
DIDN'T KNOW DAD KNEW ANY GOOD JOKES.)

I SUGGESTED DUCKY GET A MOHAWK HAIRCUT
AND A NOSE RING BEFORE WORK ON TUESDAY, AND
THEN SEE HOW NICE DAD WOULD BE.

OUR WAITPERSON APPEARED, AND DUCKY
ORDERED TWO LARGE SUNDAES WITH ALL THE
TOPPINGS.

HE WAS DYING TO TALK ABOUT WHAT
HAPPENED TO CAROL. HE SAID HE COULDN'T STOP
THINKING ABOUT WHAT I'D DONE.

"YOU'RE SO TOGETHER," HE SAID. "AND YOU
THINK I'M A SAINT? I WOULD HAVE BEEN A WRECK
IF I WERE IN YOUR PLACE."

A HERO AND A SAINT.

I LOVE IT.

I SHOULD RESCUE PEOPLE MORE OFTEN.

AS WE ATE OUR SUNDAES, WE CAUGHT UP ON
OTHER NEWS. DUCKY TOLD ME THAT THINGS WERE
STILL TENSE WITH ALEX. I TALKED ABOUT THE
GUYS IN MY LIFE. MY DATE WITH PETE. THE CALL

FROM CHRIS. AND MY BO SIGHTING, BEFORE CAROL'S CRISIS.

Ducky HOWLED. HE SAID I SHOULD GIVE OUT NUMBERS AND LET THE GUYS STAND IN LINE.

THEN HE LOOKED OVER MY SHOULDER AND SAID MY DEEPEST WISH WAS ABOUT TO COME TRUE.

WHEN I GLANCED BACK, I FROZE.

BO WAS CLEARING THE TABLE NEXT TO OURS.

DUCKY WAS TRYING HARD NOT TO LAUGH. HE ASKED WHEN I BECAME INTERESTED IN CRO MAGS, WHICH IS WHAT HE CALLS MOST OF THE JOCKS AT VISTA.

I HADN'T REALLY THOUGHT OF BO THAT WAY. BUT HE DOES HAVE REALLY MUSCLEY ARMS.

"Do YOU KNOW HIM?" I WHISPERED.

DOES HE EVER.

DUCKY INFORMED ME THAT BO'S FAMILY HAS A HOUSE IN TAHOE. THAT HIS BROTHER IS A FOOTBALL STAR AT SOME BIG UNIVERSITY. THAT BO ONCE CLIMBED THE SCHOOL FLAGPOLE ON A DARE.

WHEN I ASKED HOW HE KNEW ALL THIS, HE SMILED SLYLY.

"I JUST LISTEN," HE SAID WITH A SHRUG. "AND IF YOU PROMISE YOU WON'T GET UP AND LEAVE, I'LL TELL YOU A SECRET."

"PROMISE," I SAID.

DUCKY PUSHED HIS SUNDAE ASIDE AND LEANED CLOSER. "BO JUST BROKE UP WITH HIS OLD GIRLFRIEND."

I NEARLY FLEW OUT OF MY SEAT.

BUT A PROMISE IS A PROMISE. I STAYED PUT.

I CORNERED BO LATER. JUST BEFORE WE LEFT.

I'M MEETING HIM FRIDAY. AFTER HIS SHIFT.

MONDAY 3/30
HOMEROOM

WHY HOMEROOM?

IT IS USELESS AND STUPID. ESPECIALLY WHEN YOU HAVE AN UGLY, BORING TEACHER LIKE MR. LEAVITT. THEY SHOULD ABOLISH IT AND LET 1ST-PERIOD TEACHERS TAKE ATTENDANCE, SO WE CAN ALL GET FIFTEEN MORE MINUTES' BEAUTY SLEEP.

I'M IN A FIGHTING MOOD TODAY.

BROCK WAS WAITING FOR ME AT MY LOCKER THIS MORNING. HE SAID HE HEARD PETE TALKING ABOUT ME. ABOUT OUR DATE. HE CALLED PETE A LIAR, AND THEY ALMOST GOT INTO A FIGHT.

ALL OVER ITTY-BITTY ME.

PUH-LEEZE.

I MEAN, TALK ABOUT YESTERDAY'S NEWS.

I SHOULD HAVE TOLD HIM TO TAKE A HIKE.

BUT I DIDN'T HAVE THE HEART.

So I JUST SAID I WASN'T SEEING PETE ANYMORE AND IF HE KNEW WHAT WAS GOOD FOR HIM HE WOULDN'T BUG ME ABOUT WHO I DECIDED TO GO OUT WITH. AND I MARCHED OFF TO HOMEROOM.

NOBODY PUSHES ME AROUND.

LUNCH

I SHOULD HAVE CUT SCHOOL TODAY.

I DO NOT NEED THIS GRIEF.

WHAT AM I, PROPERTY?

I DO NOT BELONG TO ANYONE.

NOW PETE'S ALL UPSET. BROCK TOLD HIM THAT I SAID WE WEREN'T GOING STEADY ANYMORE.

WHO EVER SAID WE WERE GOING STEADY IN THE FIRST PLACE? BECAUSE OF ONE DATE?

THESE ARE HIGH SCHOOL GUYS. THEY'RE NOT SUPPOSED TO ACT LIKE BABIES.

THEY GO OUT WITH LOTS OF GIRLS. BUT WHEN THE SITUATION IS REVERSED, THEY FREAK OUT.

GET A LIFE!

I AM FED UP.
I AM GIVING UP BOYS.
AFTER FRIDAY.
I'LL GIVE BO A CHANCE.

7:37 P.M.

I DID NOT GO STRAIGHT HOME AFTER SCHOOL
TODAY. I HUNG OUT WITH DUCKY, DRIVING AROUND,
LISTENING TO HIM STRESS ABOUT HIS FIRST DAY OF
WORK TOMORROW, CALMING HIM DOWN.

HE DROPPED ME OFF AT HOME. AS I WAS
SNACKING AND LOOKING AT THE MAIL, THE PHONE
RANG.

IT WAS DAWN. CALLING ME FROM THE
HOSPITAL.

FROM MOM'S ROOM.

SHE WAS HOPING TO REACH DAD. BECAUSE
MOM WANTED TO TALK TO HIM.

I ASKED WHAT SHE WAS DOING THERE.

"JUST VISITING," SHE REPLIED.

OKAY. COOL.

THERE IS NOTHING WRONG WITH THAT.

NOTHING WRONG WITH DAWN VISITING MOM.

EVEN THOUGH SHE <u>COULD</u> HAVE CALLED ME. SHE

COULD HAVE ASKED IF I WANTED TO GO WITH HER.
I AM THE DAUGHTER. NOT HER.

But, hey, I CAN VISIT ANYTIME I WANT.
BESIDES, DAWN'S NOT REQUIRED TO TELL ME
EVERYTHING SHE DOES.

IT'S A FREE COUNTRY.

I SHOULDN'T BLAME DAWN FOR THE BAD MOOD
I'M IN RIGHT NOW.

I SHOULDN'T BE ANGRY.

I. AM. NOT. ANGRY.

TUESDAY 3/31
STUDY HALL

I STAYED AT THE SCHAFERS' LAST NIGHT. THIS
MORNING I GOT UP EARLY AND SERVED CAROL
BREAKFAST.

SHE SMILED WEAKLY AND SAID SHE WASN'T
HUNGRY.

I DID NOT LIKE THE WAY SHE LOOKED. KIND
OF DAZED AND WEAK.

I TOLD THAT TO DAWN. SHE WAS IN THE
KITCHEN WHEN I RETURNED WITH THE TRAY.

"THAT'S BECAUSE YOU BROUGHT HER WHAT YOU
LIKE, NOT WHAT SHE LIKES," DAWN SAID. "CAROL

HATES SCRAMBLED EGGS. MAYBE IF YOU TRIED A CHEESE OMELETTE . . ."

OKAY. SO I DUMPED THE EGGS AND MADE AN OMELETTE. I GRATED THE CHEESE BY HAND, THREW IN A FEW SPICES. IT TOOK FOREVER. BY THE TIME I WAS DONE, DAWN HAD LEFT. JEFF, MR. SCHAFER, AND MRS. BRUEN WERE ALL PUTTERING AROUND. THEY APPRECIATED THE WORK I WAS DOING.

I WENT BACK TO CAROL'S ROOM WITH MY GORGEOUS OMELETTE.

GUESS WHAT?

DAWN WAS WRONG.

CAROL REFUSED THE OMELETTE.

SHE DOESN'T JUST HATE SCRAMBLED EGGS. SHE HATES ALL EGGS.

MATH

HOW COULD DAWN NOT KNOW THAT ABOUT CAROL?

OF COURSE SHE KNEW IT.

SHE LIED TO ME.

SHE HATES ME.

WHY?

WHAT IS WRONG WITH THIS PICTURE?

DAWN IS MY BEST FRIEND, BUT SHE NEVER TALKS TO ME. AND WHEN SHE DOES, SHE LIES.

SHE LETS ME SLEEP OVER IN HER ROOM, BUT SHE ACTS LIKE SHE CAN'T WAIT TO GET RID OF ME.

I HELP AROUND THE HOUSE. I HELP TAKE CARE OF HER STEPMOM. BUT SHE SNEAKS OFF TO VISIT MOM WITHOUT ASKING ME TO COME ALONG.

IT DOESN'T MAKE SENSE. WHAT HAVE I DONE TO HER?

THIS IS SO UNFAIR.

SHE'S THE ONE WITH THE FUNCTIONAL FAMILY. SHE'S THE ONE WITH THE GOOD GRADES. SHE'S THE ONE WHO BELIEVES IN PEACE ON EARTH AND KINDNESS TO ALL LIVING THINGS.

SHE HAS EVERYTHING. SHE'S EVERYBODY'S FRIEND. SINCE WHEN HAVE I DROPPED OFF HER RADAR? SINCE WHEN HAVE I BECOME POISON?

I HAVE BEEN SO PATIENT. BUT I AM TIRED OF MAKING EXCUSES FOR HER. I'M TIRED OF SAYING IT'S ONLY A PHASE, SHE'S TENSE ABOUT THE BABY, ETC.

SHE DOESN'T WANT TO TALK TO ME? FINE.

TWO CAN PLAY THAT GAME.

I took a long walk. I had to clear my head.

So I went to Dad's store, to visit Ducky on his first day on the job.

He looked great. Cool haircut. New clothes. A small, conservative earring.

But after seeing him here, I have decided that Ducky's in the wrong business.

He should be in child care.

He didn't notice me at first. He was sitting on a bench in the kids' section, bouncing a couple of toddlers on his knees. They had board books in their mouths. So did Ducky.

It was so cute.

Until Dad showed up. He was not amused. I could tell by the murderous glare in his eye.

I tried to signal Ducky. He thought I was waving, so he waved both toddlers' hands back at me.

Then he saw Dad and his face paled.

Up he stood. Down went the toddlers.

"MAY I SEE YOU IN THE STOCKROOM?" DAD
ASKED HIM.

THAT WAS WHEN I LEFT.

I HATE BLOODSHED.

7:34

REPORT FROM THE BATTLEFRONT:

DUCKY SURVIVED.

MORE THAN THAT. HE WAS ECSTATIC.

DAD HADN'T FIRED HIM. JUST GIVEN HIM THE
I'M-PAYING-YOU-TO-WORK-NOT-PLAY LECTURE. VERY
POLITELY. (SURE. HE JUST SAVES HIS NASTY SIDE
FOR ME.)

ANYWAY, DUCKY LOVES THE JOB. HE THANKED
ME A MILLION TIMES. HE CAN'T WAIT FOR HIS NEXT
SHIFT, WHICH IS THURSDAY, AFTER SCHOOL. AND HE'S
SERIOUSLY CONSIDERING THE BOOKSELLING INDUSTRY
FOR A FUTURE CAREER.

I NEARLY FELL OFF MY CHAIR TRYING NOT TO
LAUGH.

I GIVE HIM, OH, A WEEK BEFORE HE CHANGES
HIS MIND.

BUT HE HAD TO CUT THE CONVERSATION SHORT.
HE WAS BEEPED BY ALEX ON CALL-WAITING.

Ducky apologized like crazy but insisted he had to talk to him.

"Oh, so Alex rates over me?" I asked.

I was joking. But Ducky took me seriously. "Come on, Sunny," he said. "Alex never calls me. This must be something important."

I told him OF COURSE I didn't mind.

Which was true.

I can't get mad at Ducky.

At least he's honest with me. At least he doesn't sneak behind my back.

Like some friends.

Which brings me to my current problem: What do I do now? Where do I go?

Where is my home base?

Everything is so different now. I mean, ever since that terrible day at Venice Beach, Dawn's family has been _my_ family. They've been the only reason I've stayed in Palo City.

But I don't feel welcome there anymore. I _know_ Dawn doesn't want me around.

Do I stay here in this empty, dirty house with dishes in the sink and laundry all over the place? With cartons of old books on the living room sofa that Dad has promised to

TAKE AWAY FOR WEEKS, BUT WHICH I KNOW I
CAN'T REMIND HIM ABOUT BECAUSE HE'LL BLOW UP
AT ME?

I HATE IT HERE.

BUT I HATE IT THERE.

WELL, EXCEPT FOR CAROL.

SHE TREATS ME LIKE A HUMAN BEING. SHE
VALUES ME.

I GUESS I SHOULD GO SEE HOW SHE'S DOING.

OH, GREAT. DAD DROVE UP.

MORE LATER.

10:34

HE MUST HAVE HAD A GOOD DAY AT WORK. OR
SOMETHING.

HE WALKED IN THE DOOR AND FOR THE FIRST
TIME IN RECENT MEMORY NOTICED THAT HIS
DAUGHTER IS A HUMAN. "WHY THE LONG FACE,
SUNSHINE?" HE ASKED.

I WAS SO SHOCKED, I ACTUALLY CONFIDED IN HIM.

I SAID THAT DAWN'S BEEN ACTING WEIRD AND
I DIDN'T THINK SHE WANTED TO BE MY FRIEND.

HIS REACTION? "WELL, MAYBE IT'S TIME YOU

STOPPED TREATING HER BEDROOM LIKE YOUR PRIVATE HOTEL SUITE."

So SENSITIVE.

THAT'S WHAT I GET FOR OPENING UP TO HIM. I SHOULD HAVE KNOWN BETTER.

WHAT'S WORSE, HE STARTED CHEWING MY EAR OFF ABOUT CHRISTOPHER — AS IN, CHRISTOPHER READS THE BOOKS THAT HE'S SUPPOSED TO SHELVE . . . CHRISTOPHER TALKS TOO MUCH TO CUSTOMERS . . . CHRISTOPHER NEEDS TO LEARN THE WORK ETHIC . . . BUT HE'S A "NICE BOY" AND HE KNOWS A LOT ABOUT KIDS' BOOKS, SO THE PARENTS LOVE HIM.

IT TOOK ME A MINUTE TO REALIZE HE WAS TALKING ABOUT Ducky.

SO NOW DAD WANTS ME TO "TALK TO HIM." I'M SUPPOSED TO GIVE HIM "WORK TIPS" AND COACH HIM ON HOW TO "USE HIS TIME EFFICIENTLY."

WHAT'S MORE, DAD'S THINKING OF HIRING ANOTHER HIGH SCHOOL KID, AND HE WANTS ME TO FIND ONE.

WHAT DO I LOOK LIKE, AN EMPLOYMENT AGENCY?

SO I'M AT DAWN'S AGAIN.

THE LESSER OF TWO EVIL HOUSES, I GUESS.

Carol's fine. She has a copy of the L.A. Times best-seller list on her nightstand and is working her way through it, book by book.

I guess I'll have to be going to the library for her.

If I can figure out where it is.

Carol, as usual, asked me all about my day. I did not tell her my feelings about Dawn, even though I was dying to. But I did mention my conversation with Dad.

She smiled. "If he needs another employee, get one of your many boyfriends a job."

Brilliant.

Why hadn't I thought of that?

I wonder if Bo wants a job.

No.

NO!

I have a much better idea.

I know just who to ask.

11:10 P.M.

Sunny, you are a genius.

Ducky thinks it's a great idea. He thinks

THIS IS JUST THE THING THAT ALEX NEEDS TO
PULL UP HIS SELF-ESTEEM.

So DUCKY'S GOING TO TALK TO HIM TOMORROW.
AND I HAVE DONE MY GOOD DEED FOR THE DAY.

APRIL FOOLS' DAY.

I WOKE UP AT THE REGULAR TIME. DAWN WAS
FAST ASLEEP. I TIPTOED TO HER DESK AND
ADJUSTED THE CLOCK TO 9:07. THEN I SNUCK
BACK INTO BED, LET OUT A LOUD GASP, AND SAID,
"OH, NO! WE'RE LATE!"

DAWN'S EYES POPPED OPEN. SHE JUMPED OUT
OF BED.

I WAS ABOUT TO YELL "APRIL FOOL!" BUT
DAWN STARTED SCREAMING AT ME — I'M LAZY, I
NEVER PAY ATTENTION TO THE TIME, I CAN NEVER
BE TRUSTED. . . .

THIS IS WHAT I GET FOR TRYING TO CHEER
UP THE MORNING?

I WAS SO DISGUSTED, I DIDN'T BOTHER TO
TELL HER THE TRUTH.

DAWN DIDN'T FIND OUT THE REAL TIME UNTIL SHE WENT INTO THE KITCHEN.

WHEN SHE DID, SHE STARTED FREAKING OUT AGAIN.

SOME PEOPLE JUST CAN'T TAKE A JOKE.

I FEEL MUCH BETTER NOW.

RESCUED BY THE SWEETEST GUY IN THE WHOLE SCHOOL.

!! BO BO BO BO BO !!

HOW CAN DUCKY CALL HIM A CRO MAG?

HE IS SO WRONG.

BO FOUND ME IN THE HALLWAY BETWEEN FIRST AND SECOND PERIODS. HE GAVE ME ONE OF THOSE LITTLE CANISTERS OF "MIXED NUTS" THAT'S REALLY A JACK-IN-THE-BOX.

HOW CORNY CAN YOU GET?

WELL, I PRETENDED TO BE SURPRISED WHEN THE SPRING POPPED OUT AT ME.

BUT I WASN'T EXPECTING THIS NOTE, WHICH WAS ATTACHED TO IT:

I am a Fool
4 U!
♥
Lookin' 4 word
2 Friday nite.
— Bo

OKAY, NOT THE BEST SPELLER, BUT WHO
CARES?

LUNCH

I AM SITTING ALONE.

BECAUSE MY HATEFUL EX-BEST FRIEND TOOK
THE ONLY EMPTY SEAT AT THE TABLE WHERE
MAGGIE AND AMALIA WERE SITTING.

SHE SAW ME HEADING FOR THAT SEAT.

I KNOW SHE DID.

I WANT TO KILL HER.

WE TALKED.

BO AND ME.

I HEARD HIS VOICE BEHIND ME AS I LEFT SCHOOL.

THE SOUND CARESSED MY EAR. LIKE THE TOUCH OF A BUTTERFLY'S WING.

I HAVE NEVER HEARD "YO" SOUND SO SEXY.

I TURNED. HE WAS HEADING TOWARD THE PARKING LOT WITH SOME FRIENDS, SO I WALKED BESIDE HIM.

HE INTRODUCED ME TO HIS PALS.

THEN HE ASKED IF SUNNY WAS MY REAL NAME.

I ASKED HIM IF BO WAS HIS.

HIS FRIENDS ALL LAUGHED.

THEN THEY CONTINUED TOWARD THE LOT. BO WAVED TO ME. HE LOOKED A LITTLE EMBARRASSED. HE MOUTHED THE WORD "LATER."

HMMMM.

IS IT POSSIBLE HE HAS A NAME MORE RIDICULOUS THAN SUNSHINE DAYDREAM WINSLOW?

TO BE CONTINUED.

11:11 P.M.

WENT TO SEE MOM TONIGHT.

GOT IN JUST BEFORE THE END OF VISITING HOURS.

I TRIED TO BUY HER FLOWERS, BUT THE STORE WAS CLOSING AND THERE WEREN'T MANY LEFT, ONLY SOME REALLY EXPENSIVE BOUQUETS. I THOUGHT ABOUT GETTING A POTTED PLANT, BUT THAT SEEMED TOO DORKY.

SO I TOOK HER A LIFE MAGAZINE INSTEAD.

AND I PUT IT ON HER NIGHT TABLE. RIGHT NEXT TO AN IDENTICAL COPY. AND A POTTED PLANT.

"ISN'T IT NICE?" MOM ASKED. "DAWN BROUGHT IT. I LOVE BEGONIAS."

REAL NICE.

DAWN SHOWS UP WITH MOM'S FAVORITE PLANT, AND I BRING A MAGAZINE SHE ALREADY HAS.

I. FELT. LIKE. SUCH. AN. IDIOT.

SHE'S EVIL.

HATEFUL.

CONNIVING.

AT THIS MINUTE, WHILE I AM IN <u>HER</u> KITCHEN, MAKING STEW FOR <u>HER</u> STEPMOTHER AND LOOKING AFTER <u>HER</u> HOUSE ALL BY MYSELF, WHERE IS SHE?

SHOPPING WITH MAGGIE.

SHE WASN'T EVEN GOING TO TELL ME. SHE WAS GOING TO SNEAK OUT WHILE I WASN'T AROUND.

AND THEN, WHEN I DID SHOW UP, WHEN I CAUGHT HER IN THE ACT, DID SHE COVER HERSELF? DID SHE INVITE ME?

NO. SHE JUST WALKED OUT OF THE BEDROOM AND INTO THE KITCHEN, WITHOUT SAYING A WORD.

MRS. BRUEN WAS IN THE MIDDLE OF A PHONE CONVERSATION. I HEARD HER INTERRUPT IT AND ASK, "WHERE ARE YOU GOING, DAWN?"

AND DAWN TOLD HER, BUT IN THIS WHISPERY LITTLE VOICE. LIKE I WASN'T GOING TO HEAR.

"ISN'T SUNNY GOING TOO?" ASKED MRS. BRUEN.

DAWN'S REPLY? "I SEE ENOUGH OF SUNNY."

<u>THUD</u> WENT MY JAW AS IT HIT THE CARPET.

Zoom went Dawn out the door.

And then Mrs. Bruen was calling to me. "Sunny? Are you going to be here for the next hour or so?"

I managed to spit out a "yes."

Mrs. Bruen appeared in the bedroom door. "Mr. Schafer just called. He forgot some important files, and he wants me to run them over to his office. But I am concerned about leaving Carol alone. If she should need anything —"

"She's not alone," I snapped.

"Is that okay with you, Carol?" Mrs. Bruen called into the next room.

"You bet," Carol answered.

Off went Mrs. Bruen, shouting a list of instructions: "Keep an eye on the stove. I've got a stew going. Listen for Carol. And call Jeff's friend Spencer. The number's by the phone. Tell him I'll pick him up on the way back."

Robo Slave Daughter back again. Same girl, different house.

And now, as if everything isn't just the absolute worst, some OBNOXIOUS JERK is blowing his horn outside.

RIGHT IN FRONT OF MY HOUSE.

I THINK I'LL THROW SOMETHING AT HIM.

SOME OF THESE TOMATOES LOOK JUST RIGHT.

6:05 P.M.

WHAT DID I DO?

A LOSER. THAT'S WHAT YOU ARE, WINSLOW. A HEARTLESS, BRAIN-DEAD, SELFISH LOSER. THE BOTTOM OF THE PILE.

WAS IT ONLY AN HOUR AGO I HEARD THAT HORN?

ONLY AN HOUR SINCE I MADE THE BIGGEST MISTAKE OF MY LIFE?

NO. THE SECOND BIGGEST. THE FIRST WAS BEING BORN.

I SHOULD HAVE BEEN BORN IN THE YEAR 3000 OR SO. WHEN THEY HAVE TIME TRAVEL. SO I COULD SLIP BACK IN TIME AND REDO ALL THE STUPID MISTAKES I MAKE.

LIKE TODAY'S.

LIKE WHEN I LOOKED OUT THE WINDOW TO SEE WHO WAS MAKING THAT NOISE AND SAW THAT IT WAS BO, PARKED IN FRONT OF MY HOUSE.

WHAT KIND OF GUY SITS IN FRONT OF A

GIRL'S HOUSE, HONKING AWAY SO THE WHOLE
NEIGHBORHOOD CAN HEAR? WHY DIDN'T HE GET OUT
AND RING MY DOORBELL?

IF HE HAD RUNG THE BELL, I WOULD NEVER
HAVE HEARD HIM. HE WOULD HAVE GOTTEN BACK
INTO THE CAR AND LEFT. AND NONE OF THIS
WOULD HAVE STARTED.

I SHOULD HAVE PELTED HIM WITH TOMATOES.
BUT NO. MY MIND HAD TO TURN INTO MEAT LOAF.
I HAD TO RUN OUTSIDE BECAUSE IT WAS <u>BO</u>.

AND WHAT DID HE WANT?

TO TELL ME HIS REAL NAME. THE NAME HE
COULDN'T MENTION IN FRONT OF HIS FRIENDS.

IT'S BEAUREGARD.

BEAUREGARD MONTFORT ROLLINS.

BECAUSE HE WAS EMBARRASSED TO ADMIT THAT
AT SCHOOL, HE HAD TO COME ALL THE WAY OVER
TO SAY IT.

AND I WAS <u>MOVED</u>. I THOUGHT HE WAS BEING
SO SWEET AND VULNERABLE TO DRIVE ALL THAT WAY
JUST FOR THAT.

SO I TOLD HIM MY FULL NAME. WE LAUGHED.
WE CHATTERED ABOUT ALL KINDS OF STUPID THINGS.

I MUST HAVE BEEN THERE A LONG TIME. I
SORT OF FORGOT ABOUT THE REST OF THE WORLD.

THEN I HEARD THE SMOKE ALARM.

My stomach fell so fast it made my head spin.

I bolted. I don't even remember if I said good-bye to Bo.

I tore across the Schafers' lawn and into the house. The pot was smoking on the stove. Inside it, the stew had become a lump of solid black.

"Sunny?" Carol called.

She was in her doorway.

Standing.

"Get back in bed!" I called out.

I turned off the burner. I almost grabbed the pot. But the handle had melted. So I found a mitt, threw the whole thing into the sink, and turned on the water.

Bad move. The moment the water hit the pot, it let out a loud hiss and the kitchen filled with smoke.

The alarm was still screeching. And now the phone and the doorbell were ringing.

"Should I call the fire department?" Carol called out.

"No!" I shouted back. "Everything's fine! Just — just go back to your room!"

I opened all the windows. I fanned the

smoke under the detector until the sound stopped.

Then I ran to Carol's room. She was lying on her bed, grimacing.

"Are you okay?" I asked.

"You told Mrs. Bruen you'd be here," she said. "I'm not supposed to move."

"I'm sorry," I said. "I just —" I couldn't finish the sentence.

"Just WHAT?" Carol asked. "Who was that boy you were talking to?"

"Boy?" I repeated.

"Yes, Sunny. I SAW you. Out the window."

IT WAS AN EMERGENCY.

AN EMPLOYEE OF DAD'S.

SOMEONE FROM THE HOSPITAL.

The lies marched through my head.

But I couldn't lie.

Not to Carol. I had to tell the truth.

"His name is Bo," I said.

"Bo," Carol repeated.

"Well, Beauregard," I went on. "Which is what he wanted to tell me. That's why he was blowing his horn. . . ."

Lame. That sounded so lame.

I wanted to melt right into the carpet.

Carol was staring at me with the strangest look in her eyes.

Fear. Pain. Disbelief. Anger. Disgust. Confusion. All of it at the same time, like flashing neon lights.

Pinning me.

Blaming me.

"So you ran outside to flirt," Carol said. "With the stove on."

"I didn't do it on purpose!"

"Look, I realize it's boring to look after an invalid. I don't like being one. I don't want to burden people. But someone else is involved in this. Someone who is depending on me to stay healthy. Someone whose life has just been put at risk —"

"I know! I said I was sorry!"

"Sorry doesn't matter, Sunny! We'll all be sorry if —"

Carol sank back into her pillows. She shut her eyes, and tears squeezed out from under her lids.

"What should I do?" I pleaded. "Should I call the doctor?"

Carol shook her head. "No. I'll do it. Just bring me the portable phone, please."

LAS PALMAS COUNTY PARK

IT IS SO DARK OUT HERE.

BUT PEOPLE ARE AROUND.

I'M NOT SCARED.

YET.

DUCKY, WHERE ARE YOU?

MAYBE HE'S NOT COMING. MAYBE HE LIED TO ME OVER THE PHONE. MAYBE HE'S DISGUSTED WITH ME TOO.

WELL, HE'LL JUST HAVE TO STAND IN LINE. BEHIND DAD, CAROL, MOM, DAWN, MRS. BRUEN, MR. SCHAFER, JEFF, AND CAROL'S DOCTOR.

WHAT IF HE DOESN'T COME? WHERE AM I SUPPOSED TO STAY NOW?

NOT AT HOME.

NOT AT DAWN'S HOUSE EITHER. NOT AFTER TODAY.

I'LL STAY HERE. I CAN SWIM OUT TO THE ISLAND IN THE MIDDLE OF THE POND. SLEEP WITH THE TURTLES. DREAM ABOUT THIS AFTERNOON.

JUST <u>SEEING</u> THAT DOCTOR WAS FREAKY. HE LOOKED SO MAD.

HE KNEW WHO I WAS. HAD TO. CAROL MUST

HAVE TOLD HIM. THE GIRL WHO PUT HER LIFE IN
DANGER.

He WAS PROBABLY MAKING THE FIRST HOUSE
CALL OF HIS LIFE. DOCTORS DON'T <u>MAKE</u> HOUSE
CALLS. ONLY IN EMERGENCIES.

I SHOULD HAVE LEFT THEN. CAROL WAS IN
GOOD HANDS.

BUT I COULDN'T. ONE ABANDONMENT WAS
ENOUGH.

So I STAYED UNTIL MRS. BRUEN CAME HOME.
WITH JEFF. BOTH OF THEM SCOLDING ME BECAUSE
I HADN'T CALLED SPENCER'S HOUSE.

<u>CALLED SPENCER'S HOUSE!</u> IF ONLY THAT HAD
BEEN MY WORST MISTAKE. I WOULD HAVE TAKEN
THAT IN A MINUTE.

I <u>COULDN'T</u> TAKE THE EXPRESSION ON MRS.
BRUEN'S FACE WHEN SHE SMELLED THE BURNING
ODOR THAT WAS STILL IN THE HOUSE. AND HEARD
THE DOCTOR'S VOICE. AND RACED TOWARD CAROL'S
ROOM, MURMURING, "OH MY GOD."

AND I ALMOST SMACKED JEFF WHEN HE RAN
INTO THE KITCHEN AND EMERGED WITH THE CHARRED,
WARPED POT.

<u>LAUGHING</u>.

BUT EVEN THEN I DIDN'T LEAVE.

I STOOD THERE LIKE A TREE, ROOTED TO THE

CARPET, UNTIL MRS. BRUEN CAME BACK INTO THE
LIVING ROOM.

HER LIPS WERE TIGHT. EVERY LAST MRS.
BRUEN-ISH TWINKLE WAS GONE FROM HER FACE.

"IS THE BABY ALIVE?" I BLURTED OUT.

"WELL, THERE'S STILL A HEARTBEAT," MRS.
BRUEN SNAPPED.

"WHEW," I SAID. "THAT'S A RELIEF."

"WHAT HAPPENED?" JEFF ASKED.

MRS. BRUEN GLARED AT ME. "WHY DON'T YOU
TELL HIM, SUNNY?"

"I'LL NEVER LET IT HAPPEN AGAIN, MRS.
BRUEN. I PROMISE."

"WHAT?" JEFF INSISTED.

MRS. BRUEN SHOOK HER HEAD. "NO, I WON'T
LET IT HAPPEN. I WAS THE ONE WITH THE
ULTIMATE RESPONSIBILITY, SUNNY. I GAVE THAT
RESPONSIBILITY TO YOU. I TRUSTED YOU. BUT I
WAS WRONG TO DO THAT. I HAVE TO TAKE THE
BLAME TOO."

"IF YOU WON'T TELL ME, I'M GOING TO ASK
CAROL!" JEFF DECLARED, STOMPING AWAY.

"I THOUGHT YOU WERE MATURE, SUNNY," MRS.
BRUEN BARRELED ON. "I NEVER, EVER IMAGINED
THAT BECAUSE OF A FLIRTATION YOU'D PUT TWO
LIVES AT RISK —"

"I KNOW! I KNOW!" I SHOUTED.

"YOU'D BETTER KNOW, SUNNY," MRS. BRUEN SAID. "BECAUSE I'M GOING TO HAVE A GOOD, LONG TALK WITH MR. SCHAFER ABOUT THIS."

NOW JEFF CAME RUNNING BACK TO US. "YOU LEFT HER?" HE SHOUTED. "WITH THE STOVE ON?"

"WELL, SORT OF —"

"EVEN I'M NOT STUPID ENOUGH TO DO THAT."

THAT WAS IT.

I COULDN'T TAKE IT.

NOT ANOTHER MINUTE.

"DO YOU THINK I'M HAPPY ABOUT WHAT I DID?" I SHOUTED. "YOU THINK I'M PROUD OF MYSELF? THAT I'M TOTALLY IGNORANT ABOUT HOW SERIOUS IT IS? I KNOW, ALL RIGHT? I KNOW I DID THE WRONG THING. I'M NOT AN IDIOT! YOU DON'T HAVE TO KEEP YELLING AT ME!"

MRS. BRUEN LOOKED LIKE SHE WANTED TO KILL ME.

I COULD NOT STAY THERE ANOTHER SECOND.

I WAS OUT THE DOOR.

A CAR JUST ZOOMED BY. SOME UGLY YAHOO WITH A STRINGY MUSTACHE LEANED OUT THE WINDOW AND SHOUTED SOMETHING UNINTELLIGIBLE AT ME.

If Ducky doesn't show up, I am out of here.

The bus station isn't too far away. I have enough money to go somewhere.

I think.

8:30

He's here.
Thank. God.

9:15
Somewhere in the Palo City Hills

I can't talk anymore. I'm all talked out.

I hate writing in a moving car, but I'm going to try it anyway. If I have to blow chunks, we can always stop.

It won't be the worst thing that happened to me today.

I do feel a little better, though.

It's all thanks to Ducky.

Ducky, who practically had to scrape me off that bench at Las Palmas because I was

SO UPSET. DUCKY, THE ONLY PERSON ALL DAY WHO HAS NOT JUDGED ME. WHO HAS NOT REMINDED ME WHAT A CRUEL, WORTHLESS PERSON I AM. WHO HAS ACTUALLY <u>LISTENED</u>.

THE FACTS, ACCORDING TO D.

1. I WAS WRONG.
BUT I ADMITTED IT.
2. SOMETHING BAD COULD HAVE HAPPENED.
BUT IT DIDN'T.
3. THE BOTTOM LINE:
CAROL'S FINE.
THE BABY'S FINE.

THE NEGATIVE SIDE? A LOT OF PEOPLE ARE MAD AT ME.

THE POSITIVE SIDE? I DIDN'T LIE. I ACTED FAST. I TURNED OFF THE STOVE IN TIME.

I DID THE RIGHT THING TO LEAVE THE SCHAFERS'. I COOLED OFF. I LET THEM COOL OFF TOO.

ANYWAY, WE WORKED OUT A PLAN. I HAVE TO GO BACK. APOLOGIZE AGAIN. CALMLY, THIS TIME. GENTLY.

JUST SIT AND TALK IT OUT. LIKE MATURE PEOPLE.

I'M SCARED OUT OF MY MIND.

DARK.

QUIET.

DEAD.

THE WORLD IS OFF. UNPLUGGED.

EVEN THE CRICKETS ARE SLEEPING.

NOT ME.

I CAN'T EVEN COME CLOSE.

MIGHT AS WELL KISS THE NIGHT GOOD-BYE.

THE SUN'LL BE UP ANY MINUTE.

THIS IS TURNING INTO A HABIT. <u>WHY IS THIS
HAPPENING TO ME?</u>

ACCORDING TO DUCKY, EVERYTHING WAS
SUPPOSED TO WORK OUT. I SHOULD BE SNOOZING
LIKE A NEWBORN.

I THOUGHT I DID EVERYTHING RIGHT.

I WENT BACK TO THE SCHAFERS'. I RANG THE
BELL.

MRS. BRUEN ANSWERED. (SHE HAD DECIDED TO
SPEND THE NIGHT.) SHE DIDN'T THROW ME OUT. IN
FACT, SHE INVITED ME INTO CAROL'S ROOM.

MR. SCHAFER WAS THERE, SITTING ON THE
BED. THEY BOTH LOOKED A LITTLE WARY. BUT THEY
LET ME SIT WITH THEM.

JEFF, FORTUNATELY, WAS ASLEEP.

DAWN WASN'T.

SHE WAS IN HER ROOM, DOING HOMEWORK.

SHE CAME IN ONCE, GLANCED AT US, THEN LEFT. NO COMMENT.

I TOLD CAROL I KNEW SHE WAS UPSET WITH ME. I SAID I WOULDN'T BLAME HER IF SHE KICKED ME OUT OF THE HOUSE.

"IT WAS MY FAULT TOO," MR. SCHAFER SAID. "I SHOULDN'T HAVE ASKED MRS. BRUEN TO COME TO MY OFFICE."

MRS. BRUEN SHOOK HER HEAD. "I SHOULDN'T HAVE AGREED."

"I AGREED TOO," CAROL ADDED.

THEY WERE TRYING TO MAKE ME FEEL BETTER. BUT IT WASN'T WORKING. THEY WERE MAKING EXCUSES. LIKE, THEY SHOULD HAVE KNOWN I WOULDN'T BE RESPONSIBLE ENOUGH.

"I'M NOT A BABY," I REMINDED THEM. "YOU SHOULD HAVE BEEN ABLE TO TRUST ME. I LET YOU DOWN, CAROL."

"SUNNY, I'M NOT GOING TO SUGARCOAT THIS," CAROL SAID. "AM I UPSET? YES. HAVE I LOST MY TRUST IN YOU? WELL, MAYBE. ONE THING ABOUT TRUST, THOUGH. IT'S RENEWABLE. BUT YOU HAVE TO EARN IT."

My eyes were starting to water. "I want to," I said.

"I know you do, sweetheart. And you'll get a chance. I just don't know how many stews we'll be making."

I smiled at her. She smiled back.

We didn't hug or anything. No big scene. But it was a start.

I offered to go home for the night, but Carol insisted I stay over. So I had tea with Mrs. Bruen and Mr. Schafer in the kitchen. I watched some tube. And finally I decided to get ready for bed.

I knocked lightly on Dawn's door and pushed it open.

The first thing I noticed was my cot. It was folded up.

All my stuff was back in plastic bags, lined up by the door.

Dawn was at her desk, reading. Not even looking up.

No explanation, not even a hello. Nothing.

The same stupid game. Freeze Out Your Friend.

Almost turned around and left. I was so sick of her attitude.

But I couldn't back out. I was on a roll. I was feeling strong. My head was clear after talking things out with Carol.

I guess I figured if I could get through THAT, I could handle anything.

So I opened my big mouth.

It was the first time I had spoken directly to Dawn in days. And I have been replaying our conversation in my head all night.

I still remember practically every word.

"Hi," I said.

"You're staying?" was Dawn's reply. Into her book. Not even a glance upward.

"Well, yeah. I wanted to, but —"

"I'm surprised they let you."

"Me too. Uh, Dawn? What happened to my stuff?"

Dawn shrugged. "I put it out of the way. I thought you were going to do your thing again."

"What THING?"

"You know. What you always do. Give up. Run away."

Low. Very low.

I was cool. I was not going to scream

AT HER. THAT WAS PROBABLY JUST WHAT SHE
WANTED.

INSTEAD, I COUNTED TO TEN IN MY MIND
AND SAID, "WELL, I'M HERE NOW, DAWN. AND
IF YOU HAVE SOMETHING YOU WANT TO SAY TO
ME, GO AHEAD. I'M NOT RUNNING AWAY NOW,
AM I?"

DAWN ROLLED HER EYES. "FORGET IT, SUNNY.
I DON'T WANT TO TALK ABOUT THIS."

"NO, I WON'T FORGET IT. WOULD YOU FORGET
IT IF I INSULTED YOU?"

"IT WASN'T AN INSULT. JUST A FACT. NOW,
WILL YOU LET ME DO MY HOMEWORK?"

"JUST GIVE ME TWO MINUTES, DAWN! THE
HOMEWORK'S NOT THAT IMPORTANT."

"HOW DO YOU KNOW? YOU HAVEN'T DONE IT."

"FINE. YOU'RE SMARTER THAN ME. YOU'RE
BETTER THAN ME IN EVERY WAY. I ADMIT IT,
OKAY? DOES THAT MAKE YOU HAPPY? NOW TALK
TO ME. I'M A PERSON. I HAVE FEELINGS. I DON'T
LIKE BEING IGNORED."

"FUNNY, I'VE BEEN THINKING THAT SAME
THING."

"I DON'T IGNORE YOU, DAWN."

"NO? YOU HAVEN'T SAID A WORD TO ME ALL
WEEK."

"Only because you haven't been talking to me. You started it!"

"I had my reasons!"

"What were they?"

"I just told you, Sunny."

"What? That I run away? Is that it? That's the reason you're acting like such a jerk to me?"

Dawn slammed her book shut and turned to face me. "Excuse me? I am not going to sit here and be attacked in my own room. You want to know why I'm angry? Fine. It is because you run away. From everything. The minute something bad happens, you escape. You've been doing it all year. First homework. Then cutting a class here and there. Then cutting school. Then that guy at the beach, Carson —"

"Dawn, Carson was ages ago. You knew what I was going through. I had to escape."

"Had to? Some people face their problems, Sunny. Some people have guts."

"Like you? Perfect Dawn, who turns her back on her friend? Some guts."

"Sunny, I bent over backward for you. I was understanding. I listened. I let you

STAY OVER. I GAVE YOU ADVICE. I WAS SO
STUPID! I SHOULD HAVE KNOWN YOU'D DO THE
SAME THING TO MY FAMILY. BECAUSE THAT'S
WHAT HAPPENS, SUNNY. WHEN YOU START
BEING SELFISH, SOONER OR LATER YOU HURT
SOMEONE. AND YOU DID IT. BIG-TIME. TO THE
MOST VULNERABLE PERSON IN MY FAMILY. JUST
ABANDONED HER. YOU DON'T CARE FOR ANYONE BUT
YOURSELF."

"I DO CARE ABOUT CAROL —"

"OH, SURE, WHENEVER THERE'S SOMETHING IN IT
FOR YOU. WHEN IT'S FUN. WHEN SHE PRAISES YOU
AND GOSSIPS WITH YOU AND CALLS YOU HER HERO.
THEN YOU WAIT ON HER HAND AND FOOT. BUT
WHEN YOU ACTUALLY HAVE TO DO SOMETHING BORING
AND UNSELFISH, LIKE WATCHING A STEW POT? OUT
THE DOOR. OUT TO FLIRT WITH SOME JOCK WHILE
THE HOUSE BURNS DOWN —"

"I SAVED CAROL'S LIFE, DAWN! HAVE YOU
FORGOTTEN THAT?"

"NO ONE HAS. YOU'VE BEEN TALKING ABOUT IT
NONSTOP. BUT WHAT'S THE POINT IF YOU TURN
AROUND AND PUT HER LIFE IN DANGER?"

"I SCREWED UP, OKAY? I KNOW IT! I
APOLOGIZED TO EVERYONE AND THEY ACCEPTED IT."

"THAT DOESN'T CHANGE WHAT YOU DID, SUNNY.

You should have been here. You had a responsibility!"

"And you didn't?"

"What are you talking about?"

"Hello? She's *your* stepmother, Dawn. Not mine. Where were *you* when this whole thing happened? What great, unselfish thing were you doing? Shopping!"

"Why shouldn't I? There were two people in the house when I left! You and Mrs. Bruen. That should have been enough."

"That's *always* your excuse. Why stick around if someone *else* can take care of Carol? I never see you taking her meals in bed. Or keeping her company when she's lonely. Or rubbing her feet or reading to her when her eyes are tired. *I'm* the one who does those things. *I'm* the one who was shopping with her when she collapsed. Why? Because her own stepdaughter is never around."

Dawn laughed. "I don't believe I'm hearing this. I must be dreaming. Sunny Winslow lecturing *me* about taking care of a parent? Stop patting yourself on the back for a minute and think about visiting your own mother for a change."

"How can I? You're there all the time!"

"Oh, Sunny, that is so lame. That is beneath you. I visit your mom because I love her. I have known her all my life. And I feel bad for her. Because I know that her own daughter feels so sorry for herself that she can't ever visit."

"For your information, I do visit my mom. More times than you'll ever know."

"Wrong. I know about them all. I've sat and listened to you complain about every one."

"You don't know what it's like, Dawn. You, with the perfect family. The cute brother. The nice, uncomplicated dad —"

"Divorced dad. You forget that little detail. Do you think that's so easy? Dealing with a new person in the house who's not my real mom but who's having my dad's baby?"

"At least you have a mom! Two of them! Isn't that enough for you?"

Dawn fell silent. She gave me a long pitying look. "I guess you want to take one for yourself, huh?"

"What's that supposed to mean?"

"Sunny," Dawn said softly, "you have a mom. Count your blessings."

Those last three words hit me like a hammer.

My head was about ready to explode.

Words were bursting up through me like lava. But they caught in my twisted throat.

I was afraid I'd throw something. Hit something. Smash a window.

I turned and ran.

I didn't stop until I was home.

I didn't even say good-bye to Carol.

                                    FRIDAY 4/3
                                    10:54 A.M.

Rise and shine.

Guess I fell asleep.

Guess I'm playing hooky today.

                                         11:23

On my way out, I found this note from Dad.

What do you know
about this young
fellow Christopher
recommended — Alex?

CLUELESS.

4:04 P.M.
VENICE BEACH

I AM NOT BO'S SLAVE. I HAVE A LIFE OF MY
OWN.

JUST BECAUSE WE KNOW EACH OTHER'S REAL
NAMES, I'M SUPPOSED TO BE ATTACHED TO HIM
FOREVER?

OKAY, I CANCELED THE DATE. I DIDN'T GIVE
HIM NOTICE. SO BIG DEAL. HE SHOULD BE GLAD
I DIDN'T JUST STAND HIM UP. WHY GET SO
ANGRY? IT'S NOT THE LAST FRIDAY NIGHT IN THE
WORLD.

I DON'T WANT TO SEE ANYONE TONIGHT.
ESPECIALLY THE GUY WHO STARTED THE WHOLE
DISASTER.

I WANT TO SIT IN MY ROOM, WATCH TV, AND
PAINT MY TOENAILS.

FOR THE REST OF MY LIFE.

                                        9:56 P.M.

TWO MESSAGES FROM DAWN ON THE ANSWERING
MACHINE. ALL SHE SAID WAS, "CALL ME BACK."

RIGHT.

WHEN PIGS FLY.

                                SATURDAY 4/4
                                    1:45 P.M.

DUCKY SAYS: "HOW DO YOU KNOW WHAT DAWN
WANTS? MAYBE YOU LEFT FORTY DOLLARS THERE,
AND SHE NEEDS TO RETURN IT TO YOU."

I SAY, SHE CAN KEEP IT.

DAWN AND I ARE OVER.

I DON'T KNOW HER.

SUNDAY 4/5
4:12 P.M.

THE WORST PART OF THIS IS, I'M CUT OFF
FROM CAROL.

I CAN'T CALL HER. I MIGHT GET DAWN. AND
THEN I'D HAVE TO HANG UP.

I MIGHT GET MRS. BRUEN OR MR. SCHAFER
OR JEFF. AND THEN I'D HAVE TO EXPLAIN WHY I
HATE DAWN SO MUCH.

BESIDES, DAWN HAS PROBABLY POISONED
CAROL'S MIND. TWISTED OUR ARGUMENT TO MAKE
ME SOUND LIKE A TOTAL WITCH.

HOW WILL I KNOW ABOUT THE BABY? WILL
SHE SEND ME AN ANNOUNCEMENT? WILL I EVER SEE
THE BABY?

FAT CHANCE.

MONDAY 4/6
SOC STUD

MAGGIE ASKED ME WHAT'S WRONG BETWEEN
DAWN AND ME. AMALIA TOLD ME THAT DAWN HAS
BEEN DISSING ME IN FRONT OF EVERYONE.

I LAUGHED.

I TOLD THEM I DIDN'T CARE.

I SAID, IF SHE WANTS TO BE FRIENDS, ALL IT TAKES IS AN APOLOGY, A LARGE DIAMOND NECKLACE, A NEW NAVEL RING, AND THREE YEARS OF PERSONAL SERVITUDE.

7:05 P.M.

MOM LOOKS AWFUL.

SHE'S NOT EATING AT ALL.

SHE SAYS THE WEIRDEST THINGS. ONE MINUTE SHE'S TALKING ABOUT SOME DUMB TV SHOW SHE'S BEEN WATCHING — <u>EVERY DETAIL</u> — IN THIS BORED, MONOTONOUS VOICE. THE NEXT SHE'S TALKING ABOUT ALL THE FAMILY TRIPS WE'RE GOING TO TAKE.

AND THEN, ALL OF A SUDDEN, SHE'S HERSELF AGAIN. LIKE A WINDOW OF HEALTH HAS OPENED UP. SHE'S GENTLE AND KIND AND INTERESTED. SHE REMEMBERS DETAILS.

SHE ASKED ABOUT DAWN. JUST LIKE THAT. OUT OF THE BLUE. "I SENSED A LITTLE TENSION BETWEEN YOU TWO," SHE SAID.

SO I TOLD HER. EVERYTHING. FROM THE BURNT STEW THROUGH THE BIG ARGUMENT.

Mom listened carefully. She joked that Mrs. Bruen should have used a microwave for the stew.

Finally she clasped my hand and said, "You'll weather this one, Sunny. You always do. I have faith in you."

"You used to say that to me all the time," I murmured.

"That's what mothers are for."

I hugged her. "It feels so good to talk to you again."

"Oh, I'm all talk. Visit me more often."

"I will, Mom," I said. "I promise."

"Really?" Mom gave me a big smile. "Well, then, aren't I lucky?"

For a moment I forgot where I was. I didn't notice the cancer and the hollow eyes and grayish skin. Mom's smile was big and blinding like the rising sun. I felt all my twitches go away and I was back home, a little girl again, curled up on the sofa with Mom, sipping hot chocolate.

"Mom?" I said.

I love you. That's what I was going to say.

But Mom had a sudden twinge. She sank back into her pillow, eyes closed, teeth grinding.

"Are you okay?" I asked.

"Bedsores," she said.

I was crashing back to earth. Back to the hospital room and the pain and the IV tubes and the white sheets and the view of the parking lot.

And I felt fifty times worse than I had before.

That's the danger in visiting Mom.

You try not to let your hopes rise, but they always do. And the higher you go, the harder you fall.

That's what Dawn doesn't see.

She can't have her heart broken at the sight of Mom's body. She can't look inside Mom's eyes and see sorrows and triumphs and scoldings and kisses and late nights and lazy mornings and country walks and long drives and plays and pottery and softball games and sicknesses and years and years and years, all gone for good but somehow still there.

I can see them. It's like they're crowded

TOGETHER IN A ROOM THE SIZE OF MOM'S SOUL.
AND THE DOOR TO THE ROOM IS ABOUT TO CLOSE.

DAWN IS SO WRONG.

I DO THINK ABOUT MOM. I THINK ABOUT HER EVERY DAY. EVERY MINUTE. I THINK ABOUT WHAT'S GOING TO HAPPEN. AND PART OF THAT THINKING IS PREPARING. ARMING MYSELF. FORMING A SHELL.

BECAUSE YOU HAVE TO. IF YOU DON'T, YOU FALL APART.

COUNT MY BLESSINGS?

IT'S NOT SO SIMPLE.

THURSDAY 4/9
5:07

HAVEN'T WRITTEN IN AWHILE. NOT MUCH TO WRITE.

DUCKY'S DOING GREAT AT THE STORE.

ALEX POSTPONED HIS INTERVIEW AND DIDN'T GIVE DAD A REASON. DUCKY'S TRYING TO GET IN TOUCH WITH HIM.

AS FOR DAWN, I SEE HER AT OUR LOCKERS AT THE BEGINNING AND END OF THE DAY. SOMETIMES WE GET DRAWN INTO CONVERSATIONS

WITH MAGGIE AND AMALIA. ONCE OR TWICE I'VE
ASKED HER HOW CAROL IS, AND SHE USUALLY SAYS,
"FINE."

WE DON'T TEAR EACH OTHER'S HAIR OUT. BUT
WE DON'T SAY MUCH.

I LIKE IT THAT WAY.

I THINK SHE DOES TOO.

AND THAT'S ALL THE NEWS.

LIFE STILL BITES. BUT IT COULD BE WORSE.

I'M NOT SURE HOW, BUT IT COULD.

P.S. I'M VISITING MOM TONIGHT.

HER BEGONIA DIED. THE ROOTS CHOKED.

SO I BOUGHT HER ANOTHER.

IT'S SMALL, BUT IT'S IN A BIG POT. SO IT'LL
HAVE ROOM TO GROW.

OVER TIME.

MOM WILL LOVE IT.

Ann M. Martin

About the Author

ANN MATTHEWS MARTIN was born on August 12, 1955. She grew up in Princeton, NJ, with her parents and her younger sister, Jane.

Although Ann used to be a teacher and then an editor of children's books, she's now a full-time writer. She gets the ideas for her books from many different places. Some are based on personal experiences. Others are based on childhood memories and feelings. Many are written about contemporary problems or events.

All of Ann's characters are made up. But some of her characters are based on real people. Sometimes Ann names her characters after people she knows; other times she chooses names she likes.

In addition to California Diaries, Ann Martin has written many other books, including the Baby-sitters Club series. She has written twelve novels for young people, including *Missing Since Monday, With You or Without You, Slam Book,* and *Just a Summer Romance.*

Ann M. Martin does not live in California, though she does visit frequently. She lives in New York with her cats, Gussie and Woody. Her hobbies are reading, sewing, and needlework — especially making clothes for children.